MY SIDE OF THE STORY

TROUBLE

⤜ AT THE ⤛

MILL

LIZZY'S STORY

PHILIP WOODERSON

KINGFISHER

Read Lizzy's story first, then flip over
and read Josh's side of the story!

Chapter One

I was heading back to the road when I first heard the coach – a rattling of wheels and tackle, a clomping of horses' hooves. I looked round and saw it approaching – black with yellow doors, pulled by two white horses.

I didn't expect it to stop, but the coachman was reining back, and as it rolled to a halt, somebody tugged down the window. I recognized Mr Grumstone, owner of Grumstone's Mill. As he opened the door I curtsied.

His son Josh climbed out behind him, wearing a fine new jacket and soft brown leather boots. I moved closer, waving at him to make sure he saw it was me. He did and he grinned. He raised a hand. He was tall, with a mop of fair hair, looking jaunty and full of good humour. I was so pleased to see him after his six months away, I forgot his grim-faced father standing there putting his hat on. "Hello, Josh," I called. "How was London?"

But I never got any answer because his father was shouting and pushing Josh out of his way. He waded towards me, shaking his stick. Then his hat blew off in the wind, and this just made him angrier, for now I could hear him more clearly. He was yelling at me,

"Little thief! How dare you? What a damn nerve, stealing *my* potatoes!"

"Oh nonsense, Father," said Josh, with a wink aimed at me. "Why should she want *your* potatoes?"

"Why else would she be in my field, son?"

"Well, why don't we ask her, Father?"

Both of them turned back to me. I could have tried to explain that I had been out for a walk along the Manchester Road, getting down in the ditches to pick a bunch of wild sorrel to put in our soup for the evening. I could have tried to explain how the rain had washed off the dusty soil, leaving nests of potatoes under the lush green plants – so tempting compared to the withered old spuds for sale in Grumstone's mill shop. But I was too scared to open my mouth, so I simply curtsied again. That was a bad mistake, because I bent forward, still holding on tight, so my apron must have gaped open.

And then Mr Grumstone came at me, raising his stick. He hit me. I stumbled and tried to escape, but he whacked at my back and my shoulders. Then he hit my calves and tried to knock me over. I let go of my grip on the apron. My precious potatoes rolled down, scattering all around me, and this made him even madder. I might have been *murdered* by him, if Josh had not grabbed him. Mr Grumstone was shouting and swearing, trying to shake him off, but he tripped and went down, with his son, in the mud. And then I just carried on running, holding my skirts round my hips, up to the top of the field where I burrowed my way through a hedge, out onto the open moor.

I ran until I fell over, head first into the bracken. I lay there, panting and gasping. I expected, any moment, to feel the sting of more blows slamming down on my shoulders, cutting across my legs. But I counted to twenty, then thirty. Nothing – I'd got away.

Rolling onto my back, staying hidden down behind bracken and heather, I stared up at the slate-grey sky and I heard the door slam on the coach. I heard the rattle of tack and the coach wheels roll on the gravel. I tried to get my breath back. I was covered in bruises; my shoulders ached. My skirts were splattered with mud and my gown was torn round the shoulder. Father would ask what had happened.

Father had worked as a boiler man, oiling and tending the engines that powered Grumstone's Mill. He had worked there for twenty-two years, only to get the sack a couple of months ago. Not for any misdeed or crime, not even for any shirking – just for speaking up for his rights at a public meeting held on Bleekley Moor. Grumstone called him a firebrand, and said he was trying to stir up unrest. And Grumstone had warned all the other owners, so Father would be a marked man, unable to find a new job in any mill in the district. No wonder I'd tried to steal Grumstone's spuds, though not to get revenge as much as because we were hungry.

Still lying on my back, I thought of my friendship with Josh. Was it all over and done with? We used to meet up on the moor. Josh had taught me to ride his pony. I'd taught him to whistle a tune, which hadn't been easy for either of us due to the gap between his front teeth. We'd even set up our own little home in a shack once used by the shepherd, up on top of Scadd Ridge. And when he had been sent away 'to finish his education' he had left me the key to the shack, so I could carry on using it when I wanted time by myself. Now Josh was back for the summer, after a wonderful time, no doubt, staying with London relations and leading a fashionable life, but he'd seen me stealing potatoes! It suddenly filled me with shame – though it made me angry too – that we'd been reduced to this.

I made my way back into town.

Chapter Two

It was starting to rain again and the whole place looked drabber than ever; the walls were all black, stained with grime, and a heavy pall of coal smoke hung over the rooftops.

We lived in Workhouse Lane and we were lucky to still be here. I worked sixty hours every week in the mill to try and keep paying the rent. My younger brother, Timmy, worked fifty. He was only nine but he worked like the other small boys, using his tiny fingers to do the jobs that adults found fiddly. For this he was paid a pittance.

The cottages in our row were reserved for the senior hands at the mill – overseers and engineers. My father had been the chief boiler man. The fact that the bailiff had not been around to turf us out of our cottage still gave me hope that Father would get his job back one day.

About twenty years ago, this had been on the edge of the town. There'd been open fields behind our cottage. But since then the mill had expanded. Mr Grumstone had doubled his workforce. And now there were back-to-back tenements behind as well as in front of us – three storeys hemming us in, cutting out much of the daylight, crowded with so many people that it was seldom quiet and never private. In the buildings across the road from us a hundred shared each privy. All the waste had to drain away down a festering open sewer – straight past our kitchen window.

The whole warren was owned by the mill. All the mill-hands had to pay rent, about a third of their wages. Most of them hated it here, but times were hard, there was no other work, so we all lived in fear of losing our jobs and having to go to the workhouse.

The workhouse was at the end of our lane. It was a gaunt, towering building. Its windows were barred like a prison. It housed two hundred poor souls – old folks, crazy people, unmarried mothers with babies and homeless little orphans too young to start work in the mill. The able-bodied worked every day grinding up bones and gristle for making fertilizer. They lived on gruel and dry bread. Married people were parted, children taken away from their mothers. All talking was strictly forbidden. The thought of that place made me shiver.

I let myself in the front gate. I saw my brother Timmy peering out of the open front door. He was back from Sunday school, from learning to read and write. Behind him I could see Father at the kitchen table, along with my uncle George.

Uncle George had come to live with us after the death of my aunt. He suffered from lung disease. He'd got it from breathing in dust at the mill. Now all he could do was stay at home, coughing his life away. He looked after my baby twin sisters when everyone else was working, and any other small toddlers left with him by their parents.

Humbert and Jimson, Father's old friends from the mill, were also here. They were both agitators for better pay and conditions – so far, strictly in secret. They'd not been caught out like Father, though it was thanks to them, I knew, Father had got involved. Now they were back from Manchester. They'd been taking part in a meeting put on by some people calling themselves 'the Chartist movement'. They were telling Father about it. None of them noticed me, so I sat down in the corner where Timmy showed me a drawing he'd done at the Sunday school. It showed a very thin man wagging a finger – Curate Broome, giving one of his lectures!

Meanwhile, I heard Humbert going on about how much they had learnt. He was praising the Chartist movement. I looked up. I must have looked puzzled, for Father caught my eye and said, "You've heard of it, Lizzy. You must have heard us before, talking over the Charter and whether it's ever likely to help us working men get better pay and conditions?"

We all wanted better pay – without holding out much hope for it. Wages had sunk to half what they were back in the 1820s. Father said that every honest man should earn enough from his labours to feed and clothe his family and put a roof over their heads.

"But what is the Charter?" I asked him.

He said it was like a petition. It demanded that every man in the country should have the right to vote, and not just property owners, as it was at the present. Thousands of people had signed it. But when it had been delivered to Parliament the Government had refused to even look at it. "So where does that get us?" I said.

"We need strong allies" said Jimson. "The Chartists have friends in high places. They'll persevere, they'll succeed in the end and get the vote for all men because that's just natural justice. And in the meantime, if we stand with them, they'll help make our voices get heard for better conditions and pay. And just think, if we do win the vote, we'll vote for men who'll stick up for our rights in Parliament, then we'll get somewhere!"

"*If...*" said Father. "I wonder."

Then Humbert went mumbling on about the man

who had spoken wanting to come to Bleekley to talk with the representatives from each of the local mills. And then it all came out. Both of them hoped that Father might host this meeting, here in our humble cottage. "Then you'll get to hear more for yourself, Matt."

What they meant was that Father had nothing to lose, not having a job any more. But Father agreed, saying he'd welcome the chance to hear the man air his views, if only to disagree. They both slapped him hard on the back.

Then Billy our lodger came in. Humbert and Jimson greeted him like the good fellow he was. We only had two bedrooms upstairs so Billy slept in the kitchen. He had to unroll a straw mattress and lie down beside the stove. Luxury, he called it, after the dark damp cellar in which he'd been sleeping before.

Now he came straight over to me, with a grin, saying he thought he'd seen me out on the Manchester road, not far from Grumstone Towers. I shook my head, but didn't say anything.

Billy was stubby and nervy, with gingerish hair. He was like an overgrown puppy. As Father said, if he'd had a tail he'd have wagged it whenever he saw me. An orphan, released from the workhouse when he was nine years old, he had been at the mill for six years, sweeping the floors and carting out waste. But now he'd got the lofty post of the manager's errand boy. He was one year older than me.

"You look like you've been through a hedge," he said.

I saw my own face in the mirror. My lip was swollen and I had a black eye. I looked down and saw my dress was ripped and my stockings were muddy.

"What *have* you been up to?" asked Father.

"Not hoping to see Master Josh?" Billy joked. "I heard he would be back here today, up on the steam train from London!"

I glared at Billy, but Uncle broke in with a great fit of coughing, excited by 'new-fangled steam trains puffing smoke like iron dragons . . .'

"You don't get progress without it. Our town makes enough," grinned Jimson.

That was true enough, but not very funny. We never knew when it was cloudy here, because there was so much smoke. Specks of soot kept falling like snow, mucking up any washing we had to hang out to dry. The sheep on the moors were stained black.

But Father would not be diverted, "Just keep well away from that Josh, girl. Remember, you promised, last autumn."

I had promised to 'keep well away' because Josh wouldn't be near, and only then with my fingers crossed. "Josh won't want to see *me*, Father."

"No, he'll be that changed," agreed Uncle, just able to stop himself coughing, "too much of a gent for us humble folks."

To try to change the subject I said I would get the supper. But what did we have? A few carrots, half a yellowing cabbage and a mouldy crust of a loaf. For soup I needed to light the stove and burn up some precious firewood and draw water up from the well. The well was our luxury here. We only had to share it with five other cottages, whereas all the folks in the back-to-backs had to make do with stand pipes which were turned on for two hours a day.

I went to the well. Billy followed. I let him haul up the bucket. I wondered what Josh might be doing right now, back with his horrible family in their great opulent mansion. I was thinking I might walk up to the shack as soon as we'd finished with supper, if only to be by myself for a bit, when Billy interrupted, as if he'd been reading my thoughts.

"The Grumstones are having a party tonight for Lord and Lady De Bris, along with their daughter, Louisa. That ought to keep Josh amused, eh?"

I couldn't hide my annoyance. "I heard that she's ugly and stupid – and she's five years older than him!"

"So what? She's got blue blood in her veins!"

"And what does that prove?"

Billy laughed out loud, delighted he'd got a reaction.

Chapter Three

It gave me a restless night thinking of my friend Josh coming home at last, and having to spend his first evening with a sow like Louisa De Bris! I had spent the best part of the winter dreaming about what he might be up to, living it up in London. But when was I likely to see him again? Would he come to the mill, I wondered?

On Monday through to Saturday we had to be up at five, to reach the mill for five-thirty. It wasn't too hard at this time of year as we could see where we were going. Though somehow having the sun in the sky, even shrouded in smoke from the chimneys, made going into the mill for the day feel even more depressing. We knew we wouldn't be out again before the sun had gone down.

We took a short cut down an alleyway, between two tumbledown slums. We joined a flow of people all trudging like us to the mill, our clogs clacking along on the cobbles. We came out at the top of the High Street. From here we headed down hill. At the bottom the millpond glittered as if it was clear and clean. In fact it was turgid with filthy waste that had drained from the open sewers. All summer it reeked like a cess pit, unable to drain away because the sluice gates were shut, restricting the flow of water to power the giant mill wheel.

We had to go over the bridge.

My brother liked to stop on the bridge to play his favourite game. He dropped a stick over one side then chased across to see it emerge on the opposite side. He got me to count and remember how long the sticks took every day. Our record was seven seconds. Today I counted to forty. I guessed the stick had got stuck. Timmy tried again. And again. By the time we got to the mill the foreman was closing the gate. We ran for it, just squeezing through. The foreman lashed out with his boot, "Lazy oafs! Want to keep your jobs, make sure you're here early tomorrow!"

It seemed so dark in the mill after the brightness outside. The lower ground floor was piled up high with giant bales of raw cotton. These were delivered on barges, all the way from the Liverpool docks. The finished fabric was shipped the same way – along the canals, across country, or back to the docks to be loaded on ships that sailed to places like India, or back to America, from where the raw cotton had come!

We climbed three flights of stairs. Up on the raised ground floor the carding machines were rattling away, straightening the raw cotton fibre. On the first floor the spinners were working, producing thick thread on their throstles and finer thread on the mules. Compton's Mules were giant machines that stretched across the whole width of the building. They thundered away so loudly they made the walls vibrate.

The looms were on the third floor. These were powered by leather belts running overhead. They made a harsh, squealing noise. I worked on one with Timmy, scrambling under the loom to repair any broken threads, and pulling the finished fabric through on the opposite side.

The only way we could talk was by shouting in each other's ears or making signs at each other. The cotton dust blocked up our noses. It coated every surface with heaps of furry grey dust. Last autumn there'd been a bad fire in here; friction between two cog-wheels had sparked a fatal explosion. It killed my aunty Maggie. She'd been like a mother to Timmy and me. It still made me sad to think of her. Since then I'd had to do my best to mother the younger children.

The air was rank with the oil they used to keep the looms shunting smoothly. The first day I came to work here, after Father was sacked, I didn't think I could bear it. But soon I adapted, like everyone else. There was no other choice – it was work or starve.

We worked for three hours until eight-thirty when

we got some breakfast – thin porridge and milk in metal cans. We only had a few minutes before we were back on the looms. The hours went by. It was nearly midday, time to stop for our dinner, when word went round with gestures and signs that visitors were approaching.

Moments later I caught sight of Jenks at the far end of the hall, a slant of greasy black hair plastered across his forehead. He was the manager here, a stooped, grey, anxious man. As the figure behind him moved forward under a hazy skylight, I suddenly saw it was Josh. The light glowed on his fair hair. He was looking relaxed, even smiling as Jenks cupped a hand to his ear as if explaining something. Any second now he'd surely see me. Then, suddenly, Timmy was screaming.

I spun round. "What's the matter?" But he was up in the air, like a man being hanged, his legs kicking. His sleeve must have caught in the belt. It had tugged him right off his feet, high up over the loom. I scrambled up onto it, grabbing his legs, trying my best to support him, screaming out for someone to stop the belt going round. Then everybody was shouting; people were rushing about. Someone was up behind me, reaching up on my left, trying to pull Timmy's hand free, but it was jammed under the wheel at the top, squashed between iron and leather. Then the belt gave a jolt and cranked back, and Timmy fell back in my arms.

We all tumbled backwards together. I was in the middle so I was fairly well-cushioned as we crashed into the floor. The impact made us roll over. I was still trying to cradle Timmy. His shirt-front was covered in blood. He was clutching one hand with the other. The darkness seemed to close over us. There were so many people that they blocked out the light. Then everything went strangely quiet. The power to the looms had shut off, leaving only the general hubbub we didn't normally hear, of machines on the floor below, rumbling away in the background. So just for a very brief moment I could hear Timmy whimpering. Then everyone else was shouting, throwing out suggestions. "Tear off a strip from the fabric!" "Make a bandage, stem the bleeding!"

A hand was patting my shoulder. I turned. It was Josh. Our eyes met. I tried to thank him, but then someone else was yelling, "What scoundrel has stopped the machinery?!"

And I knew that voice. It belonged to the man who owned this whole great mill, the man who had sacked my father and thrashed me with his stick, Josh's father, Isaac Grumstone. At once Josh turned away, stumbling back on to his feet. All the other girls were curtseying, but I was still down on the floor, half-hidden behind the loom.

Josh hurried across to his father, but Mr Grumstone kept on shouting. He wanted to know what was happening. Why were people not at their looms? Why were they standing here idle when there was graft to be done?

Jenks told him, "An accident, sir."

He never once looked our way. When his son tried to tell him that a child had been hurt, he didn't seem to care in the least. He was bawling that this was an outrage – the whole place brought to a standstill because of one careless urchin. "The fool wasn't paying attention. I'm not paying people like that in my mill. You must punish him, Jenks, dock his wages. And everyone else in the loom room too. You all should have carried on working!"

I heard Josh protest it had all been his fault, "I told Jenks to turn off the power."

"What for?"

"Because the boy's life was in danger."

His father spat on the floor. "You young fool. This is no place to get sentimental. But seeing as you're back from London, and it's your birthday this week..." He turned on his heels. "Let them off." And with that

Grumstone was gone, dragging his son behind him, leaving his manager, Jenks, to make a hasty speech on behalf of all us mill-hands, to thank Master for his great kindness...

But I wasn't concentrating. Timmy was still on the ground, doubled up, stretching his arm out as if to get the source of the pain as far away as he could. His whole little body was shaking with shock. I bent down to look at his hand. I lifted it out of a puddle of blood. For the first time I saw what had happened. Three of his fingers were missing, leaving three mangled stubs.

I thought I was going to faint at that point. I felt dizzy. I wanted to vanish. I didn't know what to do. Then one of the older women took off one of her stockings and wound it tight round his hand, trying to staunch the bleeding. We got him up on his feet.

The overseer was shouting for everyone to go back to work.

I had to get Timmy home, but I needed the overseer's gracious permission first. He had to open the doors, as these were kept locked during work-time. And then I needed to plead with him to be allowed back later on, so I'd not lose a full day's pay.

Chapter Four

Father wasn't at home. Uncle said he was out with a chain gang, picking stones for the day in one of the huge new fields being ploughed from the edge of the moor on the De Bris estate. "But what on earth's happened to Timmy?" The twins both burst into tears.

We got him out of his bloodstained shirt. Uncle lit the fire in the grate and heated some milk, while I wrapped Timmy up in a blanket and sat him in Father's chair. He complained that his shoulder was hurting too much to raise his right arm. He kept shivering. What he needed was medical help.

I went out to find Widow Julip. She was a crazy old woman, but she knew about natural remedies that came a lot cheaper than doctors and their medicines. She lived in a tumbledown cottage out of town. It was up a steep, winding footpath. She was asleep when I got to her cottage, so I had to wake her up. She wasn't keen on coming. I promised to make it worthwhile. Still grumbling, she followed behind me, bringing a jar of ointment and a bag of 'herbal infusion' she claimed would steady the nerves.

Half an hour after Julip's visit Timmy was sleeping, his hand wrapped up in a bandage made from an old, shredded shirt. I paid Julip with the only money I could find in the house – a handful of copper coins from the pot on the mantelpiece. This left us with nothing to live on until the end of the week when I'd be owed more wages. I couldn't afford to lose more time so I hurried straight back to the mill. I thumped on the door for attention.

The overseer kept me waiting, and when he did let me in he said he would have to dock me three hours' pay. I'd only been gone half that time! I cursed him. That made him laugh, enjoying his moment of power.

It was nearly nine in the evening before I got home again. I had spent seven more hours on the loom. I found Timmy wide awake. He was crying his heart out and soaked with sweat. Neither my father nor my uncle knew what we ought to try next.

"He's been like this all afternoon" Uncle said, "except when the curate was here."

I asked what the curate had wanted. It had been a charity visit, one of his usual jaunts to visit the old and the sick. He had escorted Dora Grumstone, Josh's oldest sister. She was serious and religious. Uncle said she'd come to see Timmy. "She told me, if ever we feel the need, we can go up and ask at the kitchens and there will be leftovers for us!" Uncle coughed a big gobbet of phlegm. "And Master Josh, he was hovering about, back again like a bad penny."

I felt my cheeks flush. "Back *again?*"

"Oh, didn't I tell you before? He rode down first thing this morning. Seemed to think he'd find *you* here."

I tried to shrug this off, saying he must have been just passing by, on his way to the mill, no doubt. But Father looked up from his Bible which he read every evening. He frowned as Uncle mumbled that Josh had come here for a key.

"What key would that be now?" said Father.

Uncle looked at me too. I wondered how much he knew. I crossed my fingers and murmured something about a key to a store, "Josh left it with me last summer. He must have forgotten I'd got it when he went off down to London. Now I suppose he's remembered."

"That shack on the moor, lass, is that what you mean?" Father knew how we had spent time up there, 'playing house' as he called it. He hadn't liked it one bit. "You haven't been back since, I hope?"

I kept silent, letting him guess.

"Well, you're not going there again, and that's final. It belongs to the Grumstone estate."

"But they never use it," I blurted, "and sometimes I just need space, somewhere to be by myself, where I don't have to work, or clean, or cook, or have to look after the children. And Josh *was* my friend," I added.

Father gazed at me with a more tender look in his eyes. "A childhood friend," he said softly, "but now you're both growing up and heading in different directions." He raised his craggy eyebrows. "We're hosting a meeting, remember. Men from the other mills are coming round here tomorrow to talk about standing up for our rights. I can't have the boss's son dropping in." He held out his big, blunt hand. "I'd rather you gave me that key."

"No, I won't. *I'll* send it to Josh."

He took his time to digest this. "Very well. But I'm trusting you, Lizzy."

Upstairs I found Timmy sitting up, eyes sore and wide and staring. His face looked deathly pale in the yellow candle flame. His forehead was sticky and hot. I got on with changing his bandage. The wound looked livid and inflamed. The stubs of his fingers still oozing with thick, congealing blood. The rest of his hand had swollen up to more than twice its normal size. It looked like a monstrous mauve glove. I wrapped it up and I told him to rest. Then I sat by the bedroom window.

By now it was almost dark. I thought about the old stone shack on the ridge, with its drooping, mossy tiled roof, half-buried in brambles and nettles. Inside it would be dry and snug. There were old chairs, rugs and a fireplace where we'd burnt logs to keep ourselves warm. I thought about Grumstone Towers standing alone in its park. I imagined the Grumstone family enjoying roast meats and potatoes.

But what about Josh, I wondered. Why had he come to our cottage? He couldn't have needed the key. He had a key of his own. The second time, of course, he would have been worried for Timmy, but he must have thought I would be home. Would he try to make contact again?

Much later I went back downstairs. Timmy had woken again and I wanted to mix an infusion to help him get back to sleep. Father and Uncle had gone up to bed. As I poured a little hot water from the kettle into a cup, Billy came up behind me.

"That key to the shack," he said softly. "You could give it to me, if you want to. Jenks sends me up to the Towers with the mail first thing every morning."

"That sounds very grand, but no thanks." I said. "It's none of your business, Billy."

"I'm just trying to help you, Lizzy. Don't sneer at the work I do. I'd like to think you could respect me."

"We all do, Billy. You know that."

"I don't think *you* do, Lizzy. You just treat me like a kid brother. I'm older than you, and I've got a good job. I'm making my way in the world."

I hadn't got time for this now. I had the infusion for Timmy. "Goodnight," I said, a bit firmly, and pushed my way past back upstairs. But later, lying in bed, with Timmy sweating beside me, the twins on their old straw mattress on the opposite side, I stayed awake, my head full of worries. I heard the mill clock, far away, telling the hours through the night. And I wondered if I had been acting unkind in being so short with Billy. He had always been kind to me. I guessed he had meant no harm. But I just wished he'd leave me alone sometimes. Soon I was too tired to think any more.

Chapter Five

Tuesday passed like every other day. I did fifteen hours in the mill, standing at the loom all the time except for the short breakfast break and forty minutes I had to eat my dinner of cold potato pie.

I came home to find the kitchen crowded with twelve men who represented the workers from the other four mills in the town, along with Humbert and Jimson. Uncle introduced me to a Mr Reilly who sat at the head of the table. He was a tall, gangling man with heavy bags under his hangdog eyes, and thin, expressive hands that he kept pushing together as if he was deep in prayer. The table was piled with pamphlets and rolled-up Chartist posters for putting up round the town.

"Where's Father?"

"Upstairs with Timmy," said Uncle.

Father was soothing Timmy, gently stroking his arm. His cheek was hot to the touch, his nightshirt stained and damp. His eyes were rheumy and unfocused. The air had a sweet, putrid smell.

"He woke up from a nightmare screaming," said Father. "Just look at his hand."

Timmy's hand was bulging. The bandage was off.

"He's got so agitated; he says he can't lie on his bed."

Father gave Timmy water to drink. He couldn't swallow it down. His lips were blistered, his throat too sore. "He needs more than that widow's infusion. If only I knew what to do."

I nodded, hearing Reilly downstairs. His voice had a soft, Irish lilt. He was telling the men that all the Scottish mines had now come out on strike, the miners were marching south. He said that the mill-workers ought to join them. "Let us teach the cruel bosses a lesson!"

I glanced at Father. I knew he was torn as to where his duties should take him. "You should be down there, giving your views. Uncle can look after Timmy."

Reilly must have heard me coming downstairs, but he kept spouting on regardless, arguing urgent action. "All hands should down tools on the morrow!"

"You sound so grand, Mr Reilly" I said, without even thinking about it. "You'd argue the tail off a donkey. But if you've got any compassion, help one little boy – help my brother."

Reilly frowned at me, not understanding. "What help can we give the wee boy, Miss?"

"Timmy needs proper medical help, sir. A doctor should see him at once."

"But I am no doctor."

I grasped his sleeve. The jacket was far from new, but made of expensive worsted. "We could call a doctor for Timmy if we had the money to pay him. One guinea is all it would take, sir."

"More than most of the mill-hands earn in a week," he spluttered, eyes darting sideways.

"Four times what I earn," I said gently, "but you must have private means, sir, to not have to work, but come travelling around the north, preaching your brand of goodness."

Reilly winced at this. "I do my bit, Miss. And I'll willingly help in any way I can in raising some funds for the boy. Divided by twelve of us, it is still quite a sum, though I'll stretch to offering him twice that."

The others chipped in with their pennies, even a six penny bit, and Humbert offered a shilling. Uncle counted it all up, but as he was doing so someone outside rattled the latch on the door. I realized the door had been bolted.

The men were all up on their feet before I had drawn back the curtain to see Billy's face in the window. I opened the door and turned back to the men at the table, "As for you lot…"

"The bosses have spies," interrupted Reilly, "these fellows are risking their jobs to meet here and… who is this fellow?"

Billy blinked at him. "I live here." He noticed the coins on the table. "So what's all this money? Are you gambling?"

I told him we needed a guinea to summon a doctor for Timmy, but so far we only had about a third that much. And then something very strange happened. Billy offered a contribution. He took out his purse and he counted out sufficient to make up my guinea.

"No, Billy, you can't afford it!"

He said he'd been saving tips. Grumstone's business colleagues were usually generous to him when he brought them letters. "I want to help *you!*" he insisted.

Without even thinking about it I rushed forward, hugged him and kissed him. Then Uncle was sent on his way to bring back Dr Tonkiss, the only doctor in Bleekley. I went up to tell Father the news.

Father left me with Timmy. Timmy was very excited. By the time I came down again, Father had swayed the others away from following Reilly into calling a strike. Instead he said that the bosses should get a fair chance to accept their mill-hands' demands. Father said we should write these down. Reilly agreed. "Fair wages," he said, "along with fair conditions – and every man gets the vote!"

"And Matt Sprott gets his job back," Humbert put in quietly.

They all agreed they would make a petition for all the mill-hands to sign. Reilly concluded it would then be presented on the same day, Thursday, as the Lancashire trades' representatives were meeting in Manchester. "Any questions before we continue?" Reilly asked.

"Well, excuse me for asking," said one of the men, "but where will it go, this petition? I mean, there are five mills in Bleekley, with four different owners to read it, so won't we need five petitions?"

"No, there's the beauty," said Billy, winking in my direction. "I happen to know, thanks to having my job, you can take it to Grumstone Towers. Thursday night all the owners will be there. They're having a dinner together."

"Well done Billy!" said Reilly.

Billy gave me a strange glance, half wary and half triumphant. Then I remembered how generous he'd been, paying to get the doctor, so I put all my doubts away. "Yes, very good, Billy," I murmured. "And thanks again for the money, I'll pay you back one day, I promise."

"No need," he said. "No need at all."

Chapter Six

Half an hour after the meeting broke up, Uncle came back with the doctor. He'd found his man in the George Inn. Doctor Tonkiss's breath smelt of brandy.

I'd known of Doctor Tonkiss all my life. He had trained as a naval surgeon and served under Admiral Nelson, on one of the ships of the line at the battle of Trafalgar. His proud boast was amputating twenty-eight arms and legs before the last cannon went off. Now he made the best part of his living curing people's toothache with the help of an old pair of pliers. He wasn't the best choice for Timmy. Dr Harvey would have been better, but he had a practise in Macclesfield and he only came to Bleekley to attend to his wealthy patients.

We showed Dr Tonkiss upstairs. He unwound the bandage and studied the hand. He said that the pus needed drawing, but first there was 'agitation' that needed a copious bleeding. He took out a black leather pouch and selected a surgical knife. His hand was shaking. He gripped Timmy's wrist and managed to open a vein. Blood spurted up, splashing his cheek. He took out a dirty hankie and, after he'd filled a bowl full of blood, wound it tight around the wrist. Then he prescribed cold compresses, on forehead and chest and both ankles, thrice a day for a week, "Then the boy should be perfectly fine."

He shuffled off, taking the money, leaving Timmy white-faced and faint. "Just hope it was worth it," coughed Uncle. "We're four weeks late on the rent, and we owe at the shop. We've got nothing in the pot."

Father said we could only pray.

In fact I did much more than that, what with nursing Timmy and finding time to help Father write out our petition. And next day I buried my worries by doing my level best to encourage my friends at the mill, and anyone else who would listen, to sign and support the petition. I took care that none of the overseers noticed what I was up to, for fear they'd report me to Jenks.

Other than that I worked fifteen hours and spent the next night nursing Timmy. He was still in a feverish state, either too hot or too cold. The flesh round the stumps of his fingers had turned from black to green. They smelt disgusting and rotten.

Wide awake, I thought of Grumstone chasing me with his stick, and threatening to dock people's pay because they'd stopped work to help Timmy. I thought of his daughter, Dora, offering us scraps from their table. And I thought about Josh. Would he help us?

I got up and wrote this letter:

Dear Friend (as you were last year),

I haven't heard from you, but thank you for what you did, trying to help me save Timmy. Even without that disaster we've been going through difficult times here, thanks to Father losing his job. But I tell you, he did nothing wrong.

My father is really a moderate man who wants to steer the mill-hands away from outside extremists. If you could persuade your father of this and get him to offer some help by agreeing to meet with the leaders and making some compromises, I know it would be for the best − for the mill and all who work there.

I nearly ended the letter with that, but I thought of the key in my pocket, the shack where we'd met on Scragg Ridge. Impulsively, I added:

I will be busy on Thursday night, but if you'd like to meet me I will try to be at the shack at nine o'clock on Friday evening.

I signed it:

Your friend Lizzy.

But how could I get the letter to Josh? I hadn't the money to post it. A stamp cost more than a loaf of bread, and there wasn't a crust in the house. If I took it by hand to Grumstone Towers most likely I would be spotted and somebody else would be nosy enough to open my letter and read it. I thought of kind Billy, downstairs, always eager to do me a favour. He had offered to take back the key.

I wanted to keep that key, but I soon found another old key that didn't have any good use. I put this into an envelope, wrapped up in my folded note. Next morning I gave it to Billy. And thanked him, kissing his forehead, leaving him with a smile on his face, just like a fat happy baby. And strangely I felt happy as well, convinced I had done the right thing.

Back at the mill I went at it again, cajoling more folk into signing, until the petition had so many marks from all the dozens of folk at the mill unable to read or write that I'd covered six sheets of paper. This left me pleased with myself. Not because I cared either way if every man got the vote; I wanted better conditions and pay, but more, much more than that, what had driven me on was that extra demand Humbert had tacked on at the end, requesting that Father should get his job back.

The mill-hands were in full agreement with all the demands. By end of work on Thursday more than three hundred people had signed the petition and several dozen of these had promised to come along on a march to see it was delivered. In fact, there were more like two hundred gathered outside our cottage at quarter past nine that night. They were made up of delegations from each of the five local mills. Timmy was at the window. He waved and everyone cheered him.

My father was not so hearty. Not having a job at the mill any more, he felt he had no right to come. I needed to remind him that he was the reason so many had signed and turned up to join us tonight. "They want you to get your job back!"

"There's no hope of that."

"We shall see!"

Chapter Seven

We started off down the lane with Reilly taking the lead. The sun was going down in a haze of smoke from the mills, the light tinted yellowy-mauve. We walked for a mile or so out of town to the gates of Grumstone Park.

Father could remember when this had been just a farm, with nothing but poky fields surrounded by dry stone walls. Mr Grumstone had bought the land then had the farmhouse knocked down. And over the last twenty years he had built himself a palace. To start with he had been modest enough, but he'd never been satisfied so he had extended it bit by bit, from a square and reasonable house into a sort of mock abbey. It had Gothic arches and gables. And now, his latest extravagance, just visible through the scaffolding, was what looked like a mighty bell tower. This was topped with a needle-thin spire.

The grounds had been greatly transformed as well. The stone hedges had been grubbed out and the fields turned into parkland. There were dense plantations of trees and rhododendron woods. The gardens were laid out in steps, with ornamental shrubs, descending to the new lake. There were gondolas on the water, decorated with red Chinese lanterns as if to welcome the marchers!

We marched in a long procession, ourselves at the head of the snake, drawing up in the stable yard while the tail end was still near the gateway. The courtyard was crowded with carriages. Our clogs clomped loudly on the cobbles, making the horses restless.

"We've come the wrong way," called Reilly, "this is merely the back of the place. We need to go to the front, men. We come not as serfs but as equals!"

We followed him through an archway, around the side of the house. We went past a large casement window. It was spilling out soft yellow light. I glanced in through the diamond panes. The curtains and shutters were open, revealing the dining room. A giant chandelier was sparkling over the table, holding dozens of candles. There were more candles on the sideboard, more candles over the fireplace. In our house we only burnt one at a time. No wonder the light was so bright! It lit up a long dining table, cluttered with glasses and plates. On either side were twelve people or more, arrayed in their finery, sitting back in their chairs, looking red-faced and well stuffed. At the head of this table sat Josh. And next to him was Louisa, her hair in tight corkscrew curls, like a pig with a silly hat on!

This image stayed in my mind as I was pushed

along with the crowd, round to the front of the house. Then everyone stopped on the terrace, gathering around the front door. I saw Reilly tugging the bell chain.

The door inched open. A face peered out, asking us what we wanted. I glimpsed a yellow-clad shoulder – the butler in uniform. His nose twitched as if he could smell us.

"We wish to see Mr Grumstone, not his servant," Reilly declared. "We have something special to give him."

The butler stepped back, half closing the door. He seemed to be consulting with a shadowy figure lurking in the hallway. Then he peered out again. He promised that any well-wishing card or gift from the grateful workforce could be left at the door for delivery. "Of course," I gasped. "Josh's birthday!" How could I have forgotten?

"You misunderstand," said Reilly. "We want to speak with the father, and also his mill-owning guests. We have a petition we wish to present, on behalf of their many employees!"

The butler drew back yet again. The door was slammed and bolted.

Reilly thumped on the knocker. He pulled on the bell chain. No use. His suddenly world-weary face was limp with disappointment, as if it had never occurred to him we might be refused in this way. He didn't know what to do next.

I thought of those fat, red-faced diners, I thought of Josh… and Louisa. Then I thought of my own poor father, who had worked shifting stones all day, on a couple of crusts of bread. We were ghosts at the feast. But Dora had said we'd be welcome to leftover scraps from their table. There was only one way to find out. It was anger that carried me forward.

I grabbed the petition from Reilly, with its bundle of signatory papers. I pushed my way back through the crowd. Father was calling to me to come back, but I cut round the side of the house. I found the kitchen door open.

Inside it was hot and steamy. A scullery maid approached me. She frowned at my rough old clothes. "There aren't any jobs," she said primly. I told her what Dora had promised. She sniffed that she'd have to ask cook but cook would be busy right now. I saw cook through the doorway, her feet up, eating a pastry. So I took my chance. I dodged past the maid and charged up the service stairs, with her on my heels screaming at me, until I arrived in the hallway, and then she shut up and fell back, as if she was scared of being up here without being given permission.

It was scary, like another world, the plain scrubbed wood and white walls giving way to extravagant fabrics and dark oil paintings in frames. A huge portrait over the staircase depicted Mr Grumstone. His arms were majestically folded, making him look like Jehovah. Another showed Mrs Grumstone, like a plump sugar-plum fairy. She was wearing a fluffy white dress that looked like whisked-up egg whites. I headed across the hallway, over a Persian rug. I was aiming for the doorway from which all the noise was coming.

As soon as I opened the door I wished I had stayed outside.

The diners were all standing up. They were holding champagne glasses ready to make a toast. A huge cake with fifteen candles had been placed in front of Josh. He stood at the head of the table, leaning forward, ready to puff. Louisa De Bris was beside him. She was wearing a sparkling tiara. She looked so fine in her cream silk gown, with its fashionable, plunging neckline. It showed off a jutting white bust. She had one of her fat bare arms round his waist. But worse, Josh looked right through me.

I blurted out his name. He remained blank-faced.

Behind him was a huge mirror over the marble mantelpiece. I saw myself there, reflected. Me in my dirty rags and scarf, my face smeared with grime from the mill.

It suddenly seemed plain daft that Josh should have come to our cottage wanting to meet me again. More likely Billy was right, he had only wanted his key. For Josh was a gentleman now. He was wearing a dinner jacket, entertaining Louisa De Bris who was ugly, but rich, with blue blood in her veins. And that silk gown really was gorgeous! Whereas I was nothing – just common as mud. But this only made me more desperate. I brandished the rolled up petition as if I was raising a cudgel.

But then their wretched butler grabbed me from behind. He was trying to wrestle me down. I held on tight to the scroll and the thick wad of signatory notes, but I would have ended up down on the floor except for Mr Grumstone bellowing, "Let her be!"

The butler propelled me forward.

"So what do you want?" Mr Grumstone demanded.

He was shorter than anyone else in the room, with a big barrel chest like a bird, and spindly arms and legs. His nose was like a crooked beak. His napkin was tucked in his collar, speckled with gobbets and gravy. I put the wad of papers down, on the table, for him to see, and carefully unrolled the petition, turning it round for him.

"I've not got my reading glasses." He glared at me, hard black eyes looking alert as ever, despite all the wine and rich food. "You must read it yourself, if you *can*."

I started to read, loud and clear, pausing now and again to glance at my audience. Proud ladies and hatchet-faced husbands who owned the other four mills. They all looked equally baffled.

"To pay us a fair day's pay for a fair day's labour," I stated, "not to reduce our wages but bring them back up to the level of twenty years ago when rents and provisions were cheaper. We also support the Charter, demanding all men have the vote…"

I carried on, rushing through it, only slowing down at the bit about Father getting his job back. As I read this I looked at Josh, but he had his gaze on the chandelier as if this was none of his business.

Mr Grumstone held up his hand, "Who put you up to this nonsense?"

"Nobody, sir."

"Pah!"

I tried to explain that it had been signed and approved by more than nine hundred mill-hands. I flicked through the wad of papers on which they had made their marks.

"But I can see nothing but crosses!" The speaker was a large woman wearing a diamond tiara who looked so much like her daughter I guessed this was Lady De Bris.

"Because they can't write their own names, ma'am."

"Which means," put in Lord De Bris, with a twitch to his powdered eyebrows, "they're hardly likely to have the brains to know what is good for them, are they? Let alone how to know who might best govern the country! I only know what I know about that because I spend every morning reading the newspapers – dashed hard work!"

"They couldn't *afford* newspapers," I said. I knew, because Father had told me, a tax made them cost too much. And as for learning to read, there weren't proper schools in our town – only a useless old woman who called herself a 'teacher', or Curate Broome who did half an hour teaching the scriptures on Sunday.

"But this girl can read ever so well," Dora Grumstone put in, "Who taught you?"

"My father."

Mr Grumstone gave a self-satisfied belch. He smirked at me, looking really evil, as if he'd only just realized he happened to know who I was. He turned to his son, "So then, Josh, my lad? You recognize this piece of trouble?"

But Josh didn't try to defend me. In fact he had now got his eyes shut, as if he was concentrating on leaning against Louisa. Even when his father went on, in a horrid, ranting tirade, calling me horrible names like "rat of a rabble-rouser, chip off the block, SPROTT'S DAUGHTER!"

He practically spat this at me.

"But worse, you're the same little thief I caught trying to scavenge potatoes, so don't you come lecturing me." He snatched the petition and chucked it aside, into the empty fireplace. "Get out of my house. Or else, mark my words," he jabbed a finger at me, "you dare to come back, you'll be horse-whipped!"

The butler grabbed me again, and this time had his way. Lifting me off my feet he carried me out through the hallway. Someone else opened the door. He thrust me out, over the doorstep.

I found myself sprawled on the gravel. My right knee was grazed and bruised. Father helped me back on my feet. He hugged me to cheer me up, then he wanted to know what had happened. I spilled it all out. I was crying and shaking from head to toe.

Reilly was treating himself to a drink, out of a

silver flask. He slipped the flask back in his pocket and placed his hot, sticky hand on my cheek, telling me not to fret. But then Father made things seem worse. "You know what this means?" he said gently. "Most likely you'll lose your job."

Lose my job? The thought hit home, like a fist slamming into my stomach. It was too much to take. I was shaking my head, insisting, "I haven't been sacked though, just threatened – that's all – with a whipping!"

But deep down inside I was worried. I knew what was likely to happen. The mill was huge, with hundreds of girls, yet Grumstone would carry on brooding, and even if he wasn't aware that I had a job in his mill, Jenks would know. Jenks would tell him, and Grumstone would track me down. With Uncle ailing from lung disease, Timmy with only one hand and Father being blacklisted, what income we had came from me. My only hope was that Josh would speak up. This didn't seem very likely, not now, after the way he'd ignored me. I suddenly felt really angry, then desperate and sad and hopeless. Josh had his new friend, Louisa.

Chapter Eight

At five-thirty on Friday morning, I filed into the mill with the others, ignored by the overseer. The hours ticked by in a daze. All the time I was waiting to hear down the line that Mr Grumstone had come. When he did arrive he went into his office with Jenks. Then the rumour went round that 'Master' had summoned his overseers for a meeting at midday dinner.

They came back bearing notices to plaster up on the walls, warning that any person caught trying to 'stir up trouble' would be banned from the mill forthwith. Our overseer read it out loud, so everyone understood. Straight afterwards he came over and told me I had been fired. I tried to argue, I begged him, I made myself look really stupid, but of course it could make no difference. "It's not up to me," he kept saying.

I walked home, feeling empty. Had Josh read my letter, I wondered? Or had he just torn it up? I still had the tiniest hope he might meet me tonight at the shack. At least he might want to say sorry for not being able to help me.

Father was out, picking stones, but Uncle was there as usual. He guessed that I'd been fired before I started to tell him. He sighed and coughed into a bloodstained hanky, before reciting more gloomy news about poor Timmy upstairs. "He's not himself, he's been rambling, neither awake nor asleep, he keeps calling out for his mother."

Our mother had died in childbirth, delivering the poor twins, so they'd never even known her. Two years had gone by. I still missed her, but her death had hit Timmy far worse.

"He's been talking to her," said Uncle, "as if she was here answering back. And maybe she was," he added, his tired, sad eyes going distant as if he could see her too, coming forward to meet him, from far off, beyond the grave.

I spent the rest of the afternoon sitting close to Timmy, mopping his hot, wet brow. When he was fitfully sleeping at last, I stood and looked out of the window, up towards the ridge, watching the sun sliding down in the sky until it was over the shack.

I was up there before nine o'clock, hopeless but keeping my pledge. The door was locked, as usual. Pushing my hands through the undergrowth, I found the crack in the wall where we used to hide the key or letters for one another. There was only a squirming worm. I waited for almost an hour.

The light was rapidly fading, but before turning

back to go home, I looked up at the lintel over the door. The stonework was green with lichen, except where we'd scratched it away. And here I could still see the L that Josh had carefully etched, with J alongside, and the date. 1841. That had been last year, not this year. I walked home feeling terribly sad. But worse was to come when I got there.

Father was at the table, sleeves rolled over his elbows. In front of him was a letter. For a moment I feared it had come from Josh, but the writing was formal and slanted, with a signature at the bottom sealed with a lump of red wax. "What is it, Father?"

He looked up, forlorn. "It's from Grumstone's rent collector. This is our notice, Lizzy."

"I don't understand."

"Do you not?" He swung it round so I could read it from the opposite side of the table. We were one month behind with the rent. But there was worse news as Father read:

As no member of your family is employed at the mill from today, we request vacant possession of this property, for the use of other employees.

"We're to leave by tomorrow," said Father.

"How can we, with Timmy so ill? Oh Father, I am so sorry."

He looked at me none too brightly. "It's all my

fault, Lizzy, not yours. If I hadn't spoken out at that meeting up on the moor, I'd still have a job..."

"But you did what was right."

"I didn't do what was right for you, nor for Uncle and nor for the twins. And certainly not for poor Timmy."

Billy was in the corner, watching us both intently. He did his best to cheer us up, saying "most likely, it won't happen". When Father went to the privy Billy gave me a small bunch of flowers, picked from the hedgerows.

"Oh, Billy…"

"To show I still care," he said simply.

"Where will you go," I asked him, "if we have to leave the cottage?"

He told me Mr Grumstone wanted him to lodge with the manager, Jenks. "I'll be sorry to go though, Lizzy. I'd do anything for you, you know that."

He tried putting his arm around me. I veered back out of reach.

"Just trying to be of comfort. I'm sorry, Lizzy, " he said. "I know you still think I'm beneath you, but I'm your best friend. I stay loyal. I'd make a good husband one day."

Good husband? Had he been drinking, I wondered? "You're only fifteen!"

"Time passes."

"And people grow up," I fired back.

He looked at me really fiercely. "You won't be laughing one day, when I'm the top clerk in the office."

"I'm not laughing, Billy. I'm *worried*. You're a very nice boy, I know you mean well, but I've got a lot more to worry about than what you make of your life!" And with that, I bade him goodnight, retreating up to my room. From the foot of the stairs he called up to me, in a thin wheedling tone, that he would put more money into the metal pot, so we wouldn't have to worry about having food to eat, even though we'd have no home.

I burst into tears on the bed. The twins started crying as well. Timmy groaned. He was half off the bed, his bandaged hand reaching out as if to grasp at the moonlight streaming in through the window. I pulled him back and I hugged him close. Then over his shoulder he asked me where we might end up if we had to leave the cottage. I had no answer to that one.

"Will we go to the workhouse?" he said.

Chapter Nine

It was strange to wake up in the morning and not have to go to work, but it gave me no pleasure or peace. I needed to stop myself thinking. I spent the whole morning cleaning: sweeping out the fireplace, mopping the flagstones and table and dusting the mantelpiece, as if, by doing such homely things I was making my claim to the place. The pot rattled when I moved it. Instead of being empty it contained a handful of coins adding up to nearly two shillings.

I could have gone to the mill shop and stocked up with flour, fat, potatoes and a hunk of bacon. I'd have baked us a fine pie for dinner. It would have been good for us. We all needed cheering up and we needed some proper food. But I made do with what we'd got – a withered carrot and a handful of beans, to boil up a watery soup. Better that than being in Billy's debt any more than we were already.

As Father sat down at the table to eat, I heard a firm knock on the door. I peered out of the kitchen window. I saw three men outside. One of them was on horseback, in the midst of our vegetable plot, holding a roll of paper that might have been our petition. I opened the window to ask who he was.

"We want you out now," said the man. "I have legal power. I'm the bailiff."

I drew back, trying to think, wondering what we should do.

"Just open the door or we'll smash it and you'll have to pay for the damage."

Father got up, looking tired and dull. As the door was rattled and banged on, I was making a list in my mind: bed sheets, blankets, cutlery, our few simple pots, bits of clothing, and one simple wooden chest. The table and chairs belonged here, as did the mattress and wash bowl. There wasn't much else, a few oddments. But all together enough to mean we would need to borrow a handcart, though where were we meant to take it?

One of the door panels shattered. An angry face peered in, all red flesh and bristly beard. It drew back. A hand groped through. Blunt fingers tugged back the bolt. The door swung back on its hinges. Soon our kitchen was crowded with men – big, hefty, sweaty men.

"How dare you break into my home!" Father cried.

"*Your* home?" The bearded man picked up my pan of hot soup and dropped it between Father's feet. Then everyone seemed to be shouting, and Father had raised his fist and the bailiff's men drew their truncheons. But then, in the midst of this rumpus, I heard a young voice, loud and clear, asking what was happening.

They all looked around. It was Timmy, on the bottom stair, his bandaged hand held out. His pale eyes were gummy and sightless. He looked like a child risen up from the dead.

"Can't you give us a week to find a new place? I have a sick brother," I begged them.

"That's nothing to do with us," said the man, "we do what we're told. What we're paid for."

Father shrugged at me. I took Timmy, leading him by his good hand, wondering if I should sit him down and then go back to help Father.

Instead I heard somebody call from the lane and looked round to see Mr Grumstone. He was perched like an evil raven on top of a fine chestnut horse.

I screamed at him, "Don't you realize, my brother is only ill because he was hurt in *your* mill, working for *you*? Please, I beg you. Think again. Don't turn us out!"

He looked away, over my shoulder. "You ought to have thought of your brother before joining up with your father to stir trouble up at my mill. And stealing my property too!"

Behind me the bailiff's assistants were dragging out blankets and rugs, and dumping old iron pans on the grass. "Your 'property' – you mean the potatoes?"

I'd have opened the gate and gone for him. I'd have pulled him down off his horse. But then another rider came cantering up to his side, looking excited and desperate.

Josh Grumstone. I don't think he saw me, or Timmy down with the cabbages. He was gesturing back, down the lane.

The lane was filling with people, men, women and boys and girls. They were holding banners and flags. And as they drew closer I heard them too, calling out, whistling and shouting. The man at their head was Reilly, wearing his usual limp smile.

"Mr Grumstone, a pleasure it is," he called, performing a gracious bow and removing his hat, "with your son too!"

Grumstone glared at him. "What do you want, sir?"

Reilly chuckled. "I've just come along with the throng, with folk who will soon be joining hands to campaign with your own good mill-hands. These are miners and textile workers from Scotland and over the Pennines, demanding fair pay and a vote, sir. But right now we're simply out for a walk, seeking somewhere to camp for the night. If you'd like offer the use of your park...?" Then he noticed the bailiff's men dumping our clothes on the grass. "What's this?"

"We've nowhere to go," I yelled at him.

For the first time Josh looked my way too. His eyebrows arched, his mouth opened. I called, "Won't you help us, Josh?"

But Reilly was flapping his hand in the air and then he was speaking again, in a low yet ominous tone.

"I was hoping by now you'd be using your time to think about our demands, sir. You'd have seen there is justice in them. But it seems you have turned up here today to perpetuate further injustice."

"I won't answer nonsense like that, sir."

"You won't?"

Grumstone moved in his saddle, boots twitching in the stirrups as if he was torn between answering back and trampling Reilly down. But the crowd was pressing in closer now. "I have to be tough to be fair. Lead your hoodlums away, Mr Reilly."

I heard Josh asking his father what was going on here. His father retorted by asking why Josh had bothered to follow him here if he didn't know what was happening? Josh glanced my way again, with a shrug, and this time all my frustration – and *anger* at his behaviour – boiled over in helpless rage. "You know we're being evicted," I screamed, "don't pretend you don't know it, Josh. Don't you care what goes on?

Have you changed so much?"

He swung back to his father, but Grumstone snapped his whip. "This cottage is mine. I've the law on my side."

"Take this for your law," someone shouted.

A lump of rock spun through the air, narrowly missing Josh. It went crashing into the gate, making the horses whinny. Grumstone wheeled round, with his whip raised. "Come forward the scumbag who threw that!"

He was met by a hail of stones. I ducked down behind the gate. Then I remembered Timmy. I hurried back, scooping him up. But the battle had passed us by. Chased by a barrage of sticks and stones, shouts and swearing and insults, Grumstone and Josh were retreating, galloping off up the lane with half the crowd behind them.

The rest of the crowd streamed in through our gate, chasing the bailiff's men with a few well-aimed kicks from behind. The bearded man got a hefty push, so he went sprawling down in the sewer. He stumbled out, coated in greenish-brown slime and went sploshing off up the lane.

"And now" said Reilly, wiping his hands, "we'll help you take your things back indoors. And then we must go find our campsite."

Chapter Ten

That evening Billy turned up. Somebody, probably Jenks, must have told him the bailiff's men had been driven away, thanks to Reilly. I had to tell him the bailiff's men had pocketed the coins he had left for us in the pot.

"That doesn't matter" he told me. "There'll always be more, if you need it."

"You don't earn so much…"

He looked wary, but then he told me I didn't know what he earned, and he could invest in my future, and why not go for a walk now, so we could properly talk. But I didn't want to walk, or talk.

My brother wouldn't eat. When he tried to drink he would choke instead, and most of the time he was in a strange daze, mumbling under his breath, unable to make any sense. His hand was still horribly swollen, twice its normal size. The stubs of his fingers were rotting. They stank like rancid meat. And all through that night he ranted and raved, while I lay there helpless and hopeless. I could do nothing but pray for a miracle, "Please God, save Timmy…"

I thought about nothing much else until the Thursday morning when Reilly turned up again. He was bearing a loaf of bread, fresh butter, honey and ham, insisting we share this fine breakfast before coming down into town.

"I have given the owners fair chances. We wrote a good letter to each, allowing twenty-four hours to accept our proposal for talks. But none have replied, no, they're sitting it out. They're stubborn and desperate men. To make sure the mill-hands don't get the blame for walking out, stopping production, we'll need to take desperate measures. So are we to take the crowbars and smash a few looms? What d'you think, Matt?"

"That way you'll destroy people's jobs."

"Quite right. Better deal with the engines. That way we cut power for the looms and people will have to stop working, whether they choose to or not, so no one can possibly blame them."

Father folded his arms stoutly across his chest. "And how will we 'deal with the engines'? You're meaning to smash *those*, Reilly?"

Reilly looked pleased with himself. "Well, surely the owners will fear that, and that's what we'd have to do, if we didn't have this better option. We'll take the far gentler course of pulling the plugs from the boilers, so that way they can't get up steam."

"Oh, you could do that, could you, Reilly? You'd risk getting scalded to death!"

"No, Matt. Now I know a wee bit about that, I know that it takes some skill and I know *you* could do it."

Father shifted, shaking his head: "Except I don't work at the mill."

"That's right, and there is the beauty." Reilly looked even more pleased with himself, ever so quiet but certain. "You're the only engine-man here in the town not still hand in glove with the bosses. You're on our side and we need you for this. So can we depend on you, Matthew? Bearing in mind that I saved your home from the callous hand of the bailiff?"

I went with them, down into town. The square in front of the new town hall was crowded with Scottish miners and mill-hands from other towns, waving their banners and singing. They hushed on seeing Reilly climbing up on a soap box. He gave them a rallying speech and they cheered, throwing caps in the air.

"To Grumstone Mill!" Reilly shouted.

We marched to the gates of the mill. I had expected to find them closed, but carts were still coming and going, bearing loads of coal, and the chimney was churning out smoke. But as we packed into the mill yard shutters were slammed on the windows. The doors were hastily barred. Reilly rang at the main workers' entrance, calling to those inside to open up, "for your brothers!"

Overseers were guarding the doors from within. But as Reilly called to the miners to find a battering ram a scuffle broke out inside, with shouts and cries going up. Moments later the bolts were pulled, letting the doors swing open, and all at once we were greeted by gangs of smiling mill-hands, led by Humbert and Jimson. Everyone pressed through the entrance in an unstoppable flood.

We streamed through the carding rooms, up the stairs, past the mules.

Father and I got parted. I was trapped deep in the crowd so couldn't regain my place, stuck halfway up the first flight of stairs as a cheer went out up ahead, and word filtered back that Reilly was now face to face with Grumstone!

No doubt Reilly spoke with his usual skill of justice, or fire and brimstone. Though none of us heard what was said because of the noise that came from people shouting, trying to make themselves heard above all the mill machines. Those wheels and belts were still squealing away and the mules made a juddering roar. But rumours passed back down the stairs, that Grumstone was not giving way. "Go hang yourselves!" was his message.

And whether this was true or false, a great wave of anger rose up, surging through the crowd then falling back and rebounding, with everyone pushing and shoving to get away down the stairs.

Flattening myself in a doorway I let the crush pass by. I saw Father, carried aloft by a couple of burly miners, go swaying past down the stairwell. They went out of the doors at the bottom and out across the yard, towards the engine house.

This was a huge dark place, with heaps of coal on one side, the engine on the other. Its great piston was shunting back and forth, making the flywheel turn. The wheel was so big that it filled the space, its rim coming close to the roof, though its base was half sunk in a pit. The air was acrid with smoke and steam. Two sooty-faced men with shovels were on top of one heap of coal. Others were up by the engine, leaning over the guardrail. All of them were watching, eyes wide and white in the gloom, as if they were making their minds up whether to stand and fight.

"Step down," called Reilly. "You'll come to no harm, and nor will the engine, I promise."

They faltered, but seeing Father, they all started moving at once. They scrambled down the coal heap or legged it down iron ladders, coming to shake his hand. Then Father went up by himself. He put on thick leather gloves and carried a big, heavy crowbar.

He tinkered, banged with a hammer, then he

heaved and pushed with the crowbar. A whoosh and a great rush of steam blew forth. As it churned up into a cauldron of boiling hot watery air, Father leapt back out of range. He was clutching the big brass plug.

The piston kept pumping back and forth, sending the flywheel round, but now each revolution seemed to get slower, less sure, until after five or six turns it faltered and slipped half a turn. And as the cloud of steam dispersed and the hissing noise died away, I realized the rest of the mill was also deathly quiet. Then the silence was filled by voices from back inside the mill, demanding to know what had happened.

Reilly's men were quick to explain, darting from floor to floor. They were passing on the same message. Production had been halted so everyone should feel free to come out and join their brothers. "In numbers are strength," cried Reilly. He was answered with rousing cheers.

Before long the mill was empty, the street outside a great mass of waving, singing mill-hands forming a long procession. They were setting off back through the town. Reilly was in the lead. The next stop was Huston's Mill, to smash the plugs there as well.

We visited three more mills. At each one the same thing happened. Father drew the plug, unopposed by the engine men. These men all knew my father, but I noticed they kept apart, and none of them followed our lead. They stayed behind, sullen and cautious, along with the managers, clerks, overseers and foremen, afraid of offending their bosses.

It worried me now that Father, although saving the engines from harm, was going to be a marked man. That when the strike was over and everyone else went back to work, the bosses would make him a scapegoat; then he'd never be given his job back and probably, neither would I. This meant we had nothing to gain by the strike, though also no more to lose.

By mid-afternoon the whole valley was strangely quiet and still. The sky was unusually clear, as a breeze blew away all the smoke. The sun shone down, casting shadows. Away from the crowds, one could hear birds twittering up in the trees and even leaves rustling in the light breeze. As we traipsed back from Darby's Mill, our mission complete for the day, we went past a baker's shop. We were all given rolls by the baker. Perhaps he was only afraid that we would have ransacked his shop – but everyone thanked him kindly.

It was like a new world we had entered – everyone, brother and sister, all chatting and sharing jokes. And when the road crossed the mill stream, one reckless boy stripped off his shirt and took a brave jump off the bridge. He went splashing into the water. He was followed by dozens of others. Even the older workers scrambled down the far bank to cool their feet in the mill stream. Despite all the scum on the surface and the murky mud underneath, people were splashing each other, scooping up handfuls of water, laughing out loud, feeling *free*.

We got home in the early evening, hungry and talking of supper, cheerful enough at the prospect that there would be little to eat. Only to find my uncle waiting out by the gate with tears streaming down his cheeks.

He looked at us hopelessly, shaking his head. He told us that Timmy had taken a turn. "The boy had some sort of a fit. Then he went rigid, his jaw locked, he couldn't breathe…"

We pushed past him, hurrying up the stairs. Timmy was sitting bolt upright, his eyes so wide I could see the whites visible all round his pupils. I called to him, hugged him, shook him. But there was no doubt – Timmy was dead.

Chapter Eleven

As for the next few days, the twins were too young to understand that their brother was gone forever; they thought he would come back soon. Father was silent, locked up in himself. Uncle coughed and wheezed even more. We tried to make funeral arrangements.

Because of the heat we had no time to waste, but as to the type of funeral, we had no money so we had no choice. Timmy would have a pauper's burial. His body was wrapped in a sheet. We loaded him onto a plank. We balanced the plank on a handcart. Father pushed it along with us in a line following on behind, down to the gloomy graveyard.

The soot-stained headstones tilted out at all angles and were surrounded by tall, black walls. We had to go out of the gate at the back, into a little field where all the poor souls from the workhouse ended up in the black soil.

Father dug the grave. He had to disturb other corpses – just bundles of decomposing flesh with yellow bones poking out. I helped him to lower the body. I put Timmy's rag doll in his hands. And that was the moment I finally broke, having been numb since I found him dead with his eyes wide open. I cried and

I cried. Widow Julip had to drag me away so the curate could say some prayers.

When the soil had been shovelled on top we all trooped back to the cottage, I was still shaking and tearful. We had no funeral feast. A few of our friends dropped by, though none of the neighbours from Workhouse Lane – the clerks and overseers. They had to act loyal to Grumstone.

Reilly stayed away that night too, but Humbert and Jimson came round, bringing us news of the strike. I heard it all from a distance, not caring one way or the other.

Rumours were flying about that the strikers would march down to London to occupy Westminster and force the Government to grant free votes for all men. There was even a wild piece of gossip that young Queen Victoria had been assassinated.

The Army had been called in. A regiment of horses was on the streets of Manchester. But even with soldiers to back them up, the militia was too over-stretched to keep control in the north. There was talk of 'revolution'. Had Father not been depressed as it was, this turn of events would have got him.

"Why, here's our chance," declared Jimson, "we'll get rid of the bosses forever!"

But Father poured scorn on this nonsense. "You've

been listening to Reilly too long, you hothead. The only real way out," said Father, "is by doing a deal with the owners."

Reilly turned up the next afternoon, full of his escapades in riding from town to town. He'd been visiting every mill, drumming up more support with his firebrand angry speeches.

"And where does that get us?" asked Father. "If folks can't be earning a living, they're going to be hungry tomorrow, and starved by the end of the month!"

"But the owners are under pressure as well, their profits are draining away. They're desperate to get back to business, and they know they can't force back the workers. That is why I have written again to all five, here in the town of Bleekley, to give them a second chance…"

"For what?"

"To meet up and talk out a deal. Though as for us going hungry," he plonked a sack on the table, "it won't be tonight – with this chicken!"

We looked at it in wonder. How long since we'd eaten a chicken? And this was a plump, fine bird that we could spit-roast on the fire.

Father said grace an hour later, squeezing his blunt

hands together while thanking the Lord for this meal.

"No, thank Lord De Bris!" scoffed Reilly. "The chicken came out of his hen coop!"

At once Father put the knife down, refusing to eat 'stolen goods'.

"Now, look, don't be awkward," cried Reilly, "we're into a trial of endurance. It's all about who breaks first. The bosses, backed up by their power and wealth, or us simple, starving workers? We need all the help we can get, my friend, from the Lord *and* from Lord De Bris."

But Father wouldn't be moved, either by Reilly or me. The deadlock was only broken by a sharp tap on the door and Billy sidling in, a crafty grin on his face, to find himself offered a drumstick.

"Our man with a foot in both camps," said Reilly rather slyly, his gaze slanting down on the envelope Billy had placed on the table. "Do you bring us an answer from Grumstone?"

"I think you'll be happy enough, sir," said Billy.

Reilly read it out loud:

"We, the undersigned, welcome your proposal. We agree we should have a meeting with the mill-hands' leaders in Bleekley. We hope a solution can be agreed to get all hands back to work. We suggest nine o'clock tomorrow, 12th of August, at the George Inn.

Yours faithfully,

David Cartwright, John Huston, William Darby, – and last but not least," declared Reilly, "none other than – *Isaac Grumstone.*"

He brought out his flask of whisky. "We must drink to success, Matthew Sprott. We might even get you your job back!"

I went to bed hoping and praying that things might turn out for the best. The meeting could not bring back Timmy. But if Father got his job back, there might be hope for the future.

However, I couldn't sleep. I had the whole width of the mattress I used to share with Timmy, yet somehow I couldn't stay comfortable. I heard the clock striking midnight. I heard the birds in the eaves and mice scuttling under the floorboards. And then a loud 'clack' like a gunshot.

I sat up in bed. Then it happened again, and this time I knew what it was. Something had struck the window. Moonlight was streaming in through the glass. I got up and hurried across. The pane had been cracked, top to bottom.

I looked out. The garden was empty, but out in the lane, in the shadows I saw something shift. A stray dog? Or maybe somebody's pig escaped from a cellar or shed. Or else there was someone trying to hide who had been watching our cottage.

Something caught my eye down below on the front step. It was oblong and white – an envelope. A letter! I hurried downstairs. I tried to tread lightly but I couldn't help the way the woodwork creaked. I made more noise pulling the bolt on the door. I picked up the envelope. In the soft light from the moon, I saw my name printed on it in bold black capital letters.

But before I could open the letter, a hand grasped hold of my elbow, pulling me back in the house. A voice in my ear hissed, "What's happening?"

"Oh Father." I turned, "no, it's nothing," hurriedly shoving the envelope into a fold of my night dress, too confused to know what I was hiding. "I just couldn't sleep. I came out for some air. I thought I saw something moving."

"Where? In the lane? Someone's out there?"

"My eyes were deceiving me, really…"

He grunted and drew me back in. "These are troubling times" he said simply. "Like you I can't sleep, and when you're awake the mind keeps ticking over… and things always seem much worse at night than they do in the daylight, I reckon."

He bolted the door and we went back upstairs. I

heard him get into his bed, and then, by the light of a candle I opened the letter and read it:

Dear Lizzy,

I have found out that your father will be in grave danger if he goes to the meeting tomorrow. Please do all you can to keep him away, but don't tell him who warned you.

Your friend.

Chapter Twelve

As soon as the shock had worn off, my mind started racing over what this great danger might be and who the 'friend' could have been? Not Josh, that much was certain. Which meant it must have been Billy.

But why would Billy have needed to write, why had he not told us while he'd been here? Had he heard something new after leaving, back at his lodging with Jenks?

I waited until the morning to show the letter to Father. He laughed off the danger. "That's Billy, all right. The boy is just sweet on you, Lizzy."

"He's concerned about *you* though, Father!"

"I have to go, do my duty, stick up for the other moderates!"

I couldn't argue with this, but I was still scared for him, so while he was having a wash, I hid his boots and his clogs outside in the vegetable patch. Not that it stopped him from going, it only made him late. He searched the place top to bottom before he turned on me. And when I was stubborn and wouldn't own up, he ended up borrowing Uncle's old boots. These were a size too small but he set off at once, at a hobble. I followed some distance behind.

The clock was striking nine before we reached the

town centre. Its chimes made Father stride faster, breaking into a run. He was out of sight, down an alleyway, when I heard a clatter of hooves. I glanced round to see a closed coach bearing down, pulled by two black horses being whipped on by the coachman. I had to jump out of the way.

The coach and horses swept past, throwing up dust and gravel. On its door was a coat of arms for the Manchester Constabulary. Two outriders came behind, and as they clattered past, just for an instant I caught sight of Josh, riding alongside his father. Then they were gone, round the corner, onto the Manchester Road.

What a strange way to head into town! It would mean they'd be late for the meeting. Worse, it might mean Father would turn up at about the same time. I sprinted on down the alley.

The High Street was packed with people; locals and strikers from far away, all in a boisterous mood. Father was outside the inn. Its doors were closed and guarded. Father was shouting to be let in. The guards refused. According to them the meeting could not be disturbed. "But it's not even started," I shouted, forgetting I didn't want Father to be let into the inn! "Mr Grumstone's not even here yet."

"He is!" Other people confirmed it. Both sides in

the talks had gone in – Reilly with his delegation, and each of the four mill-owners including Isaac Grumstone, along with his fine son, Josh, about twenty minutes ago. But then a boy came hurtling out from the alleyway at the side, blurting some terrible news.

"Our fellows have all been arrested – they got bundled off in a coach!"

The crowd started shouting,

"What's happened?"

"A plot…"

"We've been fooled!"

"Where's Grumstone?"

"He's still there!"

"Open that door!"

I yelled that Grumstone had left with the coach. Then somebody recognised Father. Soon people were calling his name.

"Hey, Matt, you're still with us, you lead us!"

"Where are our delegates? Save them!"

"Revenge – come on – break the door down!"

A brick was thrown, then another, smashing the downstairs windows. The crowd clambered over the sills. The landlord was begging for mercy. But the mood had now turned nasty. Chairs and tables were overturned and thrown out into the street. Bottles and glasses were smashed. Barrels were breached so the beer flowed out, and the shout went up, "Free drinks on the house!"

"Come on, Father, we must leave here."

I dragged him back down the street.

In the cottage I bolted the door. We tried to decide what to do. Father was deeply depressed. The mill-owners had betrayed us – they weren't going to compromise. Now all the other leaders would be in Manchester Gaol. They'd be sentenced on trumped up charges and transported off to Australia.

"And what about us," I demanded. I was worried that Grumstone would still be out to get Father, but he seemed not to care. He sat there reading the Bible until later on in the afternoon when we had a visit from Billy.

He brought surprising news. Reilly was back again, openly walking the streets. He had escaped from the coach, evading his pursuers by hiding in a wood. He was being escorted by gangs of toughs who vowed their lives to his cause. They had Huston's Mill surrounded, on the far side of town, and were threatening to set it on fire with all the clerks still inside it, trapped in their top-floor office.

Billy reckoned that Grumstone had gambled on

the strikers losing their nerve as soon as their leaders were taken, thinking it would be 'like cutting a monster's head off!'

"The crazy fool," muttered Father. "Now the moderates have all been arrested, there's only that mad man, Reilly!"

"And you, Matt," wheezed Uncle. "You're still a free man, so Grumstone will be out to get you – and what's more, he'll know where to find you!"

"Which is why we should leave here," I added.

"There's nowhere for us to go, lass."

I thought of the shack on the ridge. I still had the key in my clothes chest. I blurted this out to Father. "We'd be safe there, at least for the next few nights…"

"I'll help," said Billy. "I'll carry your things."

"You won't." Father gazed at him sternly. "You no longer live with us, Billy. Your place is with Mr Jenks."

"You know you can trust me," said Billy, glancing my way.

I nodded, but Father kept shaking his head, as if he reserved all his trust for God, and everything else was a mystery.

Chapter Thirteen

We spent the night together on old mattresses, inside the old shack – Father, Uncle, the twins and myself.

I even slept a while, waking up before dawn. I watched the sun coming up.

The morning passed with nothing to do but keep the twins amused and look out of the pokey window. The view stretched away on both sides, up and down the valley, with Grumstone Towers on the left, the mill directly below, and the town spread out further west, under a grey sooty haze. None of the mills were working, so there were no fumes from their chimneys. Instead, there were palls of smoke hanging over the blackened rooftops where buildings had been set on fire.

The High Street was crowding with people. They looked like thousands of ants, moving in thick grey columns from the town hall, down the High Street. They were heading for Grumstone's Mill. They were gathering outside the gates.

Then Billy came. He sat beside me, trying to pat my arm and asking how I was feeling. "We're fine" I said, none too brightly. Then I asked him, "What's happening in town?"

He said the mob had been out all night, looting

shops and smart houses. Huston's Mill had been set on fire. Reilly was whipping up mayhem.

"But what brings *you* here?" Father asked him. "If you're still with Mr Grumstone you shouldn't keep coming to see us. Just leave us in peace. You've no right here."

Billy looked airy and… stupid. "I'll always be Lizzy's friend, Mr Sprott, no matter how much she scorns me. And as for Mr Grumstone, he's accused me of being a traitor, for warning you off that meeting, according to him, that what he thinks. Now he's told me I'm sacked, so don't mock me."

I couldn't think harshly of Billy. We wouldn't be here if it wasn't for him, as I now pointed out. "It was brave of you writing that letter, leaving it on the step."

"Aye, that it was," agreed Father, grudgingly, nodding his head. "Though you should have warned all the others as well, not just done a favour for Lizzy."

Billy blinked. "You still got that letter?"

I pulled it out from my apron. "Of course!"

He snatched it and read it through as if to remind himself what it had all been about, then stuffed it into his pocket. "It might be best if I keep it."

"Why?"

"I'd not want it used against me."

"I thought you'd already been sacked though?"

"But only on supposition."

"You still want to get your job back?"

"I don't want to starve," he said fiercely, his eyes dancing back and forth. Then he suddenly gripped Father's wrist. "The point is… why I came up here… it's just that it doesn't seem right, you hiding and running away, leaving the field to extremists. You've been a force for good in the town. Now bad men will burn down our mill and we'll never get any work any more. You've got a duty, you know that, to go down and speak common sense. The locals, they'd listen to you, sir."

I was stunned by his change of tone. "What's Father supposed to tell them?"

He turned to me, calm but certain. "Reilly's trying to gear up for a fight. He's holding a meeting midday outside the gates to the mill, a big one for all the strikers coming from all around. This whole thing could turn very nasty. Your father should be there and argue for peace. To take him on, point by point."

"It might not work."

"If it doesn't, at least he'd have a clean conscience."

I turned to Father. I felt afraid. "Why can't it be somebody else?"

"There is no one else," put in Billy. "They've all

been arrested, remember?"

And this was true. It could not be denied.

"I'll be there, midday," Father murmured.

Father set off in good time, refusing to let me go too. He wore a determined expression, but he was quiet, his eyes were moist when he gave me a farewell hug. No, not farewell, I reminded myself he was going to come back again shortly and then we would have to start talking about where to go from this place.

As soon as he'd gone I was restless. Uncle was keeping the twins amused – chuckling away, playing catch, his back to me as I slipped from the shack and made my way over the ridge.

I wouldn't disobey Father, but I needed to be by myself, and also to see what was happening, from closer in to the town.

From a rocky outcrop I had a good view of the town towards Grumstone Towers. A single figure was down on the road, running towards the park gates. He vanished behind some trees. Several men were riding across the park. I soon made out Mr Grumstone, with his manager, Jenks, by his side. Behind them were two other men in uniforms, constables probably. A gang of gardeners and household staff had gathered, guarding the gateway. They were armed with pitchforks and scythes. Josh didn't seem to be with them. Then I noticed the runner again, on the last straight. It was Billy.

Mr Grumstone manoeuvred his horse, bringing it broadside on, leaning down from his saddle to hear what Billy was saying. Billy pointed back at the town then up towards me on the ridge. I ducked my head down but kept watching. Now Mr Grumstone was waving his whip across in the other direction, shaking his head about something. Then he was questioning Billy, and Billy was shaking his head. Then Billy was raising his hands, fingers wide, as if insisting on something. Then he rummaged in his satchel and brought out what looked like letters – passing them up to Grumstone as if this would answer the problem. And all at once I felt cold inside.

Grumstone read each of the letters. As he read them his shoulders slumped.

And then, like a sad sort of comment, I heard someone blowing a horn. Grumstone and Billy both heard it as well. They both turned and looked up the road. The sound was repeated: Ba-*baaaa*... ba-*baaaaa*... like a hunting horn on a fine autumn day when the gentry were out chasing foxes. It came from up the valley, from some way beyond the park, yet only a little later it echoed back loud and clear, back over the town from the east.

85

I looked to the west, up the Manchester Road. Emerging from the shade of the trees was a long line of figures in red – a posse mounted on horses, with others on foot close behind. There was a whole stream of men – fifty, sixty, marching along in a column.

Again, I heard the horn blaring, answered again by that echo. And this time I looked to the east, over the roofs of the town, to where the Manchester Road dipped down on its opposite side. And this time I knew for certain it wasn't an echo of what I had heard. A second column of soldiers in red was closing in from the east. My heart lurched. I thought of Father, by now in the midst of the crowds, while the town was being surrounded. He would be trapped, they would all be trapped, unless I could get there and warn them.

Chapter Fourteen

I shouted a few words to Uncle, across the open ground. Then I was off, sprinting down the track that led down to Workhouse Lane. The puzzle of what Mr Grumstone might have been reading about slipped right out of my mind, replaced by my fear of those soldiers. I had to reach Father, and quickly.

From here, on an ordinary day, it would have taken five minutes to get to Grumstone's Mill. But this was no ordinary day. Coming out of the alleyway onto Mill Approach Road, I was caught in a seething mass of hundreds of men and women, all pushing towards the mill. I had to keep heaving and shoving. I found myself near the mill shop. It had been looted and wrecked. Smoke billowed out of the windows, forming a thick white curtain hiding the rest of the street. The rabble drew back from it, rubbing their eyes. I carried on, holding my breath.

Another dense crowd was on the far side. Some of the men had coal picks, others had axes and crowbars. A bit further on, I bumped into some girls who had worked with me on the loom floor, but no time to stop and chat.

I carried on, taking a detour down an empty side street. It took me to a dead end. I scaled a rickety fence, coming down in a bed of brambles. I waded across to a crumbling brick wall. I managed to scramble over, coming down hard on my hands and knees, on the edge of the oblong 'square' where the meeting had started already.

The spiky tops of the mill gates were visible on the far side over an ocean of heads. Reilly was up on a soap box. I could just about hear him too – his lilting Irish voice telling us this was our one big chance to make a brave bold new beginning.

"Why wait to be driven like sheep back to our prisons of toil? Men should not starve for their deepest beliefs, they should fight while they have strength! We have no need of these 'owners'! I call them exploiters… OPPRESSORS!"

There were wild cheers and shouts, "Burn, burn!"

But I could see Father now, a short way across from Reilly. He was holding his hat in the air, doing his best to be heard. And others were shouting, "Make way for Sprott. Let him have his say. He's our leader." Then two local men, good honest fellows, bore Father aloft on their shoulders.

Now Father was calling for order and calm. He called for us to do nothing but what was lawful and peaceful. "Robbing from other poor men like ourselves can only bring shame on our cause! By our actions shall we be judged!"

There was cheering, but also booing, slow hand-clapping, whistling, more cheers. I shouted but he couldn't hear me. I had to get closer, to reach him, if I was to warn him in time. "The soldiers are coming, Father!"

But I was too late. They were here.

The news spread fast through the crowd. That redcoats were in the High Street, marching towards the mill. They were coming in massed battalions, knocking aside anybody too slow to get out of their way. They used the butts of their rifles on old men, women and children. A tide of frightened people was pushing back into the square.

But as they fell back on the right, trying to squash into the square, the crowds on the left were resisting; protesting they couldn't make way because their only escape route was blocked by other soldiers forming up in Mill Approach Road. "So fight them we must!" cried Reilly.

His men were brandishing cudgels and knives. The miners held up their picks. Needing to see what was happening, I scrambled back onto the wall. There were more soldiers in the back lane, with bayonets fixed on their rifles.

I swung round, shocked, still on top of the wall, ready to jump back down. But now I could see to my left and right, far over the heads in the crowd. Two ranks of soldiers had now formed up, blocking this end of the High Street. The front rank went down on one knee. And both ranks raised their rifles.

I looked to the left. Mill Approach Road was blocked by another strong force, with two lines of infantrymen backed up by soldiers on horseback. The officers had their swords drawn. In their midst was another man not wearing a uniform, who seemed to be trying to get through. Not Mr Grumstone but Josh – as if he was taking command.

Oh, how I hated him now!

But the colonel was cantering forward. I knew he must be the colonel from the epaulettes on his shoulders and a gorgeous plume on his cap. He unrolled a large sheet of paper. He started to read out loud. His voice had a harsh barking tone, but I couldn't hear what was said until, sensing something was happening, the crowd fell gradually quiet. And then I caught a few words. "Disperse at once, go peacefully, or by the Queen's command..."

Somebody shouted, "You porker!"

The colonel broke off and with his sword in the air, tossed the paper aside. And before anybody could have any chance of moving this way or that, or even think about it, the colonel brought his sword down, barking an order to fire.

The soldiers fired from both sides, with two tremendous volleys, disappearing in whirls of blue smoke.

The crowd was convulsed. There were agonized screams as bodies went tumbling down and people were trampled underfoot as others tried to escape, pushing in all directions.

I jumped down from the wall. I was aiming myself towards the spot where I had last seen Father. I feared he might have been hit. Then the horsemen were wading in, clearing a path towards Reilly. I caught just a glimpse of Father down on his knees trying to shield a child who was clutching her own shattered leg.

I tried not to step on the bodies, but somebody shoved me sideways, and I tripped over a woman who tried to grab at my skirt. Then I slipped on the bloodstained cobbles then crawled on my hands and knees.

Ahead of me, soldiers on horses were cutting their way through the crowd. And now I saw Reilly down on the ground. His right arm was raised to protect his face. The colonel slashed him with his sword. I suddenly knew he would strike Father next. But I wouldn't let him, I'd stop him.

I lunged forward, grabbing the colonel's left boot. I hung on, dragging him sideways, yelling for all I was worth. He tried to knock me aside with his sword but I smacked at his horse's rump. The horse reared up and I lost my grip. His boot kicked me hard on the chin. And then I was down on the ground again, rolling onto my back, and I thought I was going to be killed then, trampled under his horse's hooves.

A shadow was blotting out most of the sky. I thought it was death closing in. Then a hand swooped down from somewhere behind. Somebody else had grabbed me! I was being pulled up by the collar, up over a big chestnut mare, then dumped down very roughly, over the front of his saddle.

I squirmed about, screaming wildly. But the hand pressed into the nape of my neck, forcing my head right down so the blood rushed into my head. And before I passed out I saw squiggles and stars and I heard a voice in my ear – a voice I strangely recognized – telling me to stop struggling, "I'm getting you out of this place."

Now flip over and read
Josh's side of the story!

TROUBLE
~AT THE~
MILL

JOSH'S STORY

READ LIZZY FIRST
THEN READ JOSH

KINGFISHER
An imprint of Kingfisher Publications Plc
New Penderel House, 283-288 High Holborn
London WC1V 7HZ
www.kingfisherpub.com

First published by Kingfisher 2005
This edition published by Kingfisher 2006
2 4 6 8 10 9 7 5 3 1

A CIP catalogue record for this book
is available from the British Library.

ISBN-13: 978 0 7534 1355 5
ISBN-10: 0 7534 1355 8

Printed in India
1TR/0206/THOM/SGCH/80/STORA/C

MY SIDE OF THE STORY

TROUBLE

⊷ AT THE ⊶

MILL

JOSH'S STORY

PHILIP WOODERSON

KINGFISHER

Have you read Lizzy's side of the story?
If you haven't, flip back and read it first; if you
have, you can now read Josh's side of the story!

Chapter One

"Thief!" Father shouted. "Stop, coachman!"

What on earth was he talking about? We were in our carriage, on the last leg of our journey home to Grumstone Towers. He was tugging the window open, pointing across a drab field.

The light was dismal and grey, a heavy rain cutting sideways. I vaguely made out a hunched figure – some poor little waif who'd got lost?

The coachman reined back the horses.

Father grabbed at the door catch. "She's been stealing my dratted potatoes!"

"Calm down, Father, what does it matter?" My tone was careless, contemptuous. I couldn't imagine how Father could get himself so worked up. "Surely if she wants potatoes she'd buy them in town. Far less trouble."

"She'd have to part with some money that way – money that's rightfully mine; seeing as it was my men grew those spuds, on my own land, for *my* workers to go and buy in *my* mill shop!"

"But Father, *we* don't need her money."

"Hah! It's the principle of it. It's only by me making profits that you got to go down to London!"

With that he leapt out of the carriage, shouting and waving his stick.

I followed him into the field. The girl had a shawl round her head, but next moment she called my name, and I knew that voice. It was Lizzy! She was small and wiry, with long dark hair, a pale face and startling blue eyes. She'd been quite a friend of mine once. But Father was after her, jumping the ditch and charging across the field.

She turned and ran but he followed. And I chased after them both, trying to catch up with Father before he could do any harm. He was lashing out with his stick, whacking her over the shoulders and round the backs of her legs. I lunged forward, wrenching the stick from his hand. We wrestled and lost our balance. He went down flat on his back and I came down on top.

Now Father was puffing and blowing. His face was puce, as if he was having a fit, "The damn, thieving little vermin. Who is she? You don't know her, coachman?"

The coachman helped Father back to the coach, denying he had any knowledge.

I'd almost forgotten about her myself. She was six months younger than me but had always seemed just as grown up, perhaps because she spent so much time mothering her younger siblings.

Before going south I had not been to school. I'd

been educated at home by a withered old private tutor who was always crunching up cough sweets. I never once played with the boys from the town. Most of them stank. They had head lice. My meetings with them were limited to the odd unfortunate ambush when I had to run for my life, ducking their sticks and stones. But Lizzy was more like the best sort of boy, fun to be with; she took risks. I taught her to ride my pony. She taught it to jump over hedges. Of course, she was never asked back to 'The Towers' and I never went to her cottage, though her father – our engine man, Matthew Sprott – was much respected by Father.

Instead we met up on the moor. The moor was our hiding place. Last summer we'd camped in a shack on our land. Father had never been up there. It was thanks to the butler finding out about our friendship and having a word with 'Master' that Father made up his mind to give in to Mother's most deeply held wish and send me to Clerkenwell College. Her brothers had been to school there.

Mother was born in London. Her father had been a clergyman who came from a prosperous family, so he can't have been too pleased at being sent north to Bleekley. My mother must have been my age when he took over the parish. Four years later she was unlucky enough to fall in love with my father. My eldest sister

was born the next year. My second sister came one year behind. Then I came along, the son and heir, to be followed by two more daughters.

Back in the carriage again, we passed through the gates into Grumstone Park, and set off along the wide carriageway that led to Grumstone Towers.

My father was mighty proud of 'The Towers'. They were still only two-thirds complete, with the third and final tower encased in scaffolding. It all looked so horribly new, compared to the mellow old houses owned by my uncles and aunts. The trees were mere saplings, the lawns newly sown. The gardeners were still at work digging out flower borders. We drove up to the pompous front porch which was the size of a small Gothic chapel. The indoor staff filed out of the door and as we got out of the carriage they all had to curtsey or bow.

"Go and find your mother and sisters, Josh. Your mother will be keen to hear about her brother and all his brood, living it up down south. I've work to attend to," said Father. "We've got guests coming over this evening. Officers, Josh, from the Army."

I turned to him, showing surprise.

"There's been a whole detachment," he said, "camped up at Castle de Bris. And very welcome they've been, I must say. There's been some unrest in

the neighbourhood; radicals stirring up trouble. Nothing like soldiers to make them shut up. We don't want our mill-hands infected."

This rather cheered me up. I should get the chance to play billiards with the officers after dinner. But Father was striding into the house, leaving me with the servants. First there was Lockley, the butler, saying how sorely he'd missed me. Then Mrs Veeny the cook, protesting I'd 'shrunk to a wee thin scrap' in need of roast beef and plum pudding. "We'll soon build you up, Master Grumstone!"

Leaving Lockley to deal with my luggage, I crossed the entrance hall and entered the smaller day room. It was empty but I could hear voices from behind the connecting doors into the larger drawing room.

I found my mother and sisters sitting in a half-circle around the marble fireplace, all patiently embroidering the very same piece of tapestry they had been hard at work on before I went away.

My second sister Emily jumped up to give me a hug. She was older and taller than me. The younger ones, Constance and Clara, put out their tongues and threw cushions. Even Dora, the eldest, came and kissed my cheek, leaving my mother stranded, half-buried in tapestry.

Of course, they all wanted to hear about my

excitements in London. I told them about the fine houses and streets, the brass band in Regent's Park, the theatres and plays, London fashions, and all the latest gossip about the social scene. I left out any mention of horrible Clerkenwell College. I had all my sisters enraptured. But while I was still telling them about the great modern inventions of gas lamps and railway stations, I found myself interrupted. Mother said, rather rudely, "Can't you tell us about your cousins, dear, and how were your uncle and aunt?"

I sat down in a fit of pique. I only cheered up when the maid brought us tea – cream scones and éclairs, and my favourite, a very rich chocolate cake. And while I was taking my fill of all these I must have mentioned what Father had said, about officers coming to dinner. Dora told me their visit was cancelled.

"They had to march off," said Emily, "to Manchester – *such* a waste."

"It isn't," said Constance, the youngest. "They didn't talk to any of us, only to you all the time!"

"Oh dear, sweet Lieutenant Muldoon – I'm missing him madly already!"

"Emily!" Dora scolded. "You're too young to say such things!"

"But what makes it worse," said Emily, ignoring

her serious sister, "is that we're still going to have to put up with Lord and Lady de Bris. They're coming tonight with their daughter!"

The young ones both groaned, "Loooo-*eeee*-za!"

"Don't be nasty, she's sweet," said my mother, as if this was very important. And with that she thrust the tapestry into Emily's lap, and went stomping off to see Father.

I went up to wash and get changed. Lockley had unpacked my clothes and laid out a clean shirt and suit ready for me, on my bed.

On impulse I opened my bureau, and wrote a short letter to Lizzy. Very amusing it was as well, congratulating her on escaping from Father's potato madness and suggesting we ought to meet up. I took it down for the messenger boy. "Billy, you still lodge at Sprott's?"

"Yes, sir."

I gave him a sixpenny piece. "Take this to Lizzy Sprott, if you please, but make sure that no one else sees you."

Chapter Two

Lord and Lady de Bris were half an hour late. This got Father agitated. He was pacing the hall with his timepiece. He thought that they were late on purpose – to show they were doing a favour to us, agreeing to eat our dinner. "Damn aristocrats. We're as good as them, Josh. Our mill's worth six times their castle!"

"So why invite them, Father?" I quipped.

"*Because* of their castle, you fool! Two thousand acres with four hundred yards of frontage onto the river – plenty of space for a brand new mill, with plenty of water to power it. No idle consideration with coal prices what they now are!"

"You mean if they wanted to sell?"

"Lord de Bris has got gambling debts."

When Lockley announced their arrival, Lady de Bris sailed in like a great stately galleon, towing her husband behind. He was tall and thin but stoop-shouldered, more like a crooked beanpole topped with a dusty grey wig. He'd been a dandy in Regency times and still wore a Regency tailcoat, white breeches and shoes with gold buckles. As for 'Loooo-*eeee*-za', bouncing behind, she was three years older than me. Very plain and plump, I thought, though with an extraordinary bosom.

The rest of the evening was flat. The food wasn't bad. We had ham and pea soup, baked halibut, roast chickens and rack of lamb. Then a fat rib of beef, Yorkshire puddings, cheese tarts and rhubarb pie. Father had brought out the finest French wines to try to impress the de Bris. But every time I ventured to speak, to tell them more about London, Louisa leant forward, making wide eyes, and this was very distracting.

I was glad when the ladies retired, swishing off to the drawing room, leaving us men at the table. Lord de Bris started reminiscing about the good old days of his youth, when London had been 'worth seeing'. Nothing was any good any more. "We are living through terrible times."

"Why, what's so bad?" I asked lightly.

"The fashions these days, they're just not what they were."

Father made an odd growling sound. "It's the slump in trade that worries me more. And the discontent in the workforce."

That got them both ranting on about 'Chartists' wanting to get the vote for all men. "The ignorant fools," declared Father, "the only men with the right to a vote ought to be property owners – we hold a stake in the country. As for this other nonsense, about

13

laying down the law about how we treat our own workers – it's up to me, not the government, what I pay them and how hard they work."

"Like a farmer milking his cows," said de Bris. "Besides, why pass laws to *change* things? Laws ought to keep things as they are."

Father lit an enormous cigar. Lord de Bris helped himself to more brandy, sighing about the state of things leading to revolution, "…and the guillotine, just like in France!"

"Not if the Army acts boldly," said Father, smacking his fist on the table, "if we are provoked we should strike back hard and no nonsense."

All stick, no carrot, I thought. I'd kept my silence thus far, but wanting to keep my end up, I said in a casual way that if only the 'anti-corn law league' managed to get its way there wouldn't be any tariffs on importing corn from America, "and if there's cheap wheat then the common folk could have cheap bread to eat, and then they'd not need to keep making a fuss about how much they get paid."

Lord de Bris made a strangled yelp.

"But the boy is damn right," cried my father.

"Right, sir? Ye gads!" gasped His Lordship, wig slipping back on his head. "Our farmers would lose their home market. They couldn't compete and they'd

go under. Then who'd pay my rents? I'd be ruined. I'd have to sell Castle de Bris!"

To which Father puffed out cigar smoke, forming a perfect circle.

Chapter Three

The morning was bright and clear and I was up bright and early, out in the stable by half past eight, saddling my new chestnut mare. Father had bought her specially to greet me on my return, as an early birthday present.

She proved a good easy ride. I cantered along the ridge thinking about last night – Louisa de Bris making wide eyes at me. She was older than me, she was dim, and she looked like the back of a carthorse. Though as Emily pointed out (as a joke), Louisa was an only child, the heir to a fine stately home. No thanks. When the time was right, I'd make sure I got a real beauty!

Reaching our shack I looked all about, surprised at not finding Lizzy. In my letter I'd given both time and place. How odd, I thought, keeping me waiting. I rode on down the track, hoping to meet her halfway. The moorland was purple with heather. All the squalid mess of the town was hidden by smoke from our chimneys, looking like mist from this distance. One would never have guessed it existed, except for a low rumbling noise. I turned into Workhouse Lane.

Her uncle was outside their cottage, watering his vegetable plot. He looked uneasy at seeing me there.

"Good morning, my man," I said warmly.

"May I ask, what do you want, sir?"

I didn't know what to say. But then I remembered the key Lizzy still had to my shack. It seemed like a useful excuse for coming here after her. "If you could just ask her to bring it out now?"

He shook his head, miserable man. And with that he turned away, telling me over his shoulder that she wasn't here, nor her father. "She works at your mill, Master Grumstone."

I rode home feeling puzzled about her taking a job, though also slightly relieved to know why she'd missed our appointment. As to her stealing potatoes, the mystery thickened. If she had a job she'd surely got money for groceries!

I was home in time for breakfast at ten, hungry after my outing. I managed a large bowl of porridge followed by bacon and eggs, sausages, several lamb cutlets, a helping of kedgeree and plenty of toast and butter. But while I was settling back, thinking of taking a rest, Mother asked me what I was planning to do, to keep myself busy today. I said I had books to read. Then Father said, "Not this morning, you're coming with me to the mill."

The mill was ten minutes by carriage. We went

through the town, down the High Street. The mill buildings straddled the river like a great sprawling bridge, with the water backing up behind, forming a wide, swirling mill pool.

The larger part was on the far side, topped by a towering chimney. This had been built in the last ten years. It was powered entirely by steam.

I could hear the beam engine chugging from here. It sounded like a great beating heart and lungs, sending up gasps of smoke. Until ten years ago all the power had come from water turning the giant mill wheel in the older building. But water was unreliable as a means of constant power. At least, that was what Father said, trying to make conversation – it depended on plenty of rain. Even in average weather, the water level would fall before the end of a day, stopping the paddles from turning. And as I knew very well, in times of drought the water dried up, leaving a septic sludge of filthy festering sewage, festooned with dead rats and pigeons.

The main entrance was in the new building. It had classical columns on either side and crouching lions by the doorstep. Only ourselves, the senior staff and important visitors were ever allowed to use it. Up above was a wooden clock tower, housing a large brass bell. I remembered, before I'd gone away, my mother

was always complaining about it waking her up at half past five in the morning when work began at the mill. It tolled again for the workers' breakfast break, again for their midday 'dinner' and lastly in the mid-evening, at the end of the shift, while we were eating our dinner.

We climbed several flights of stairs, Father stopping at doors on each floor to peer through the small glass panels: "Just checking that there's no slacking." Then back again, down to the first floor, to go in the general office. A couple of dozen clerks were standing at desks, writing ledgers. It was studious and quiet in here. On the left was the manager's office, my father's was on the right.

The manager hastily joined us. "Good morning, Mr Grumstone, sir. What a pleasure – your son and heir! How has school been, Master Joshua? You're fluent in Latin and Greek?"

"Fat lot of use if he is," Father sniffed, "it won't help us turn a good profit. I've brought him to see his inheritance. But tell me the news. What's been happening?"

Jenks said that a gang of fresh Irish hands had arrived from the Liverpool docks. He had put them to work in the warehouse, shifting the bales of raw fibre.

"Very good." Father jerked his jaw. "Now Josh, I'm

going to get Jenks to give you a tour round the mill. I know you've been round it before, but this time pay some attention. It's where the brass comes from that paid for you to go down to London."

"Yes, Father."

Chapter Four

Jenks took me down to the basement. It was dark as a pit, like Hell, with creatures toiling away, pushing carts, tipping them out, gathering raw cotton fibres and blending them into rough spools. The spools were then lugged to the carding room where the yarn could be straightened and stretched. Jenks kept up a running commentary, his mouth pushed close to my ear: "Now up to the 'drawer room', Master Josh, and on to the bobbin minders."

In the 'drawer room' dozens more wretches with bandy legs and white faces were busy feeding the yarn into drawing machines which gave the yarn a loose twist. Urchins with nimble fingers were winding the thread onto bobbins ready to be transported up to the main spinning room.

The noise was too deafening for Jenks to explain, no matter how loud he bellowed. The wheels and cogs made a harsh drumming sound. The leather belts overhead added a shrill angry squealing. The frames made a loud shunting noise. But worst of all was the damp, heavy heat and the thick, choking dust from the cotton.

I couldn't imagine how any sane man could stand it for more than ten minutes, yet this place was

crowded with stunted brutes who lived with it day after day. I said this to Jenks in the corridor. He brushed it aside with a smirk. "The cotton needs damp and warmth, sir, and as to the noise, that's a blessing – it stops any idle gossip. Now let's move on, see the next stage."

We watched the employees Jenks called 'the winders' preparing the warp by hand, winding it onto a beam. Then I was shown the other poor souls called 'drawers', who threaded the warp through 'eyes' on a harness structure, ready to go on the looms.

The looms were on the third floor. They were smaller than spinning machines. There must have been several dozen. Old crones were keeping them going, with little brats scrabbling round, pulling the fabric through, 'young tenters' as Jenks described them. His lips curved into a grin, showing his teeth, which were crooked and brown. "They have to look out if the yarn breaks then wriggle down under the looms and tie it together again."

Before I could think about this, I heard a loud bang and a jolt. Then screaming from the far end, with a voice piping up, "Help us, mercy! His sleeve has got caught in the belt, sir!"

Sure enough, the little rascal had been wrenched right off his feet, tugged up towards the rafters where

he swayed about, kicking and thrashing, like a fish on a hook.

A young woman scrambled up onto the loom. She was trying to grab the boy's legs. It was Lizzy! I ran down the aisle to help. I heaved myself up behind her. And as I was taller than her, I did my best to stretch my arms up to the top of the belt to disentangle the boy's sleeve, while she held him tight round the waist. But his hand was being mangled, between the wheel and the belt.

"Stop the power," I yelled.

"We can't do that, sir." Jenks sounded appalled. "It's for all the looms in this hall."

"So stop the whole hall!"

"If you say so."

Moments later, the belt gave a jerk and rolled back. Then the boy tumbled down, tilting backwards, knocking us both off the loom. We ended up down on the floor.

For a moment all was quiet. Then everyone seemed to be shouting except for the boy. Was he dead? His eyes were wide open with pain.

I knew who it was — Lizzy's brother! Why did *he* have to work at the mill? I patted his arm to console him. He screamed at the top of his voice. His shoulder was dislocated. Then I saw his hand. It was carnage.

Then my father turned up. He started shouting, wanting to know why the power had been cut.

I hastily got to my feet. I was fired by the fear of my father catching sight of Lizzy and wanting to beat her again. But instead he was threatening to dock people's pay, because they'd had to stop working.

"There's been an accident, Father. A boy might have lost his whole hand!"

"A boy's hand's worth nothing to me," Father snapped, "not if he don't pay attention. I can't have careless idlers here in my mill. Costs me brass."

I told him it was my fault that the power had been turned off. "You can't blame these people, Father."

He huffed and he puffed and he finally said he'd let them all off this time, but only because I was here, and it was my birthday in two days' time, as if that could make any difference, "Let that be the end of the matter!"

Moments later, the wheels were turning again. The belt stretched tighter and started to roll, pushing the looms back into action.

I looked down at Lizzy, still crouched on the floor. She was trying to dress Timmy's hand. I wondered if there was a doctor here, but it was too noisy to ask, and Father was tugging my sleeve. "Come, lad. Downstairs, to my office."

In the office he sat at his desk, immersed in his papers again, as if Timmy's ghastly accident had just been a brief interruption, and now it could all be forgotten. I tried to talk about it, but he shook his head. "Not now, lad."

I was too shaken to argue. But in the outer office I stood looking out of the window. And down in the bustling mill yard, I caught sight of little Timmy being escorted out, with only Lizzy to help him.

"Do you get many accidents here, Jenks?"

"Yes, of course," he said, "every week, sir."

Chapter Five

Father had business in Manchester later on in the day so I walked back to Grumstone Towers. The streets were deserted at this time of day. Everyone able-bodied was toiling away in the mills. The town seemed almost civilized, except for some ragged old people and street urchins playing with hoops.

I found Dora in the small drawing room, alone with the tapestry work. I told her about the accident and Father not being concerned. "Timmy should go to a doctor. I don't understand," I told Dora, "why all the Sprotts need to work at the mill, and why was Lizzy pinching potatoes?"

She gave me a curious look. "London's made you so pompous, Josh. Quite frankly, you understand *nothing*."

"Oh really?" I bristled. "Explain then."

Dora told me how Matthew Sprott had been fired. He'd been out of work for months, with only his children working to stop the family starving.

All sorts of ideas crossed my mind. "Fired for attending one meeting? He could have just said he was sorry and Pa would have taken him back!"

"Sprott's a man of principle, Josh."

"Stubborn, like our dear father."

"The Sprotts would have been booted out by now, Father was so annoyed, but somehow I made him see reason and let them stay in their cottage. As long as the rent gets paid, why not?"

"You're a very good person, Dora."

She sniffed, sounding just like Father. "When you see how people live in this town, we could make *so* much difference…"

"We do, we give work!" I said hotly.

She shook her head sadly. "It's hardly a gift. If you want to know a bit more, Josh, to really know what it's like here, come with us this afternoon. Every Monday, Curate Broome and I go on our charity visits."

It sounded dire. Then I had an idea. "Perhaps we could visit Lizzy?"

We made an unlikely party. Dora and I rode our fine chestnut mares, with the curate in between us, on an old piebald pony. He was dressed in a shabby grey suit. His trousers were brown with dirt. On his head was a wide-rimmed clerical hat that shaded his thin, pimply face. He told me how delighted he was to find me 'taking an interest'.

Leaving our horses at the George Inn, we ventured down narrow alleyways with tenements on each side.

They were built back to back, with three storeys, reeking of damp and decay. Ragged clothes had been hung out to dry on lines strung in between them. We went up dark, dirty stairwells, entering dark, cramped rooms. We found sick old people wheezing away, surrounded by mildew and filth. It really was very depressing.

But there was worse: we went down some steps into a squalid cellar with a soft, squelchy floor made of damp, ripe manure. The beams in the ceiling were all so low we had to move forward bent double. On the left was a pig with its snout in a trough; on the right was a rough straw mattress with a woman and three little children nestling in one corner.

The woman had 'lost' her husband, he'd been too fond of his gin. One night he had missed his turning and ended up drowned in the sewer. This left her with nothing to live on and nowhere to go but the workhouse – a place she feared more than death, she said, for they'd separate her from her children. Dora gave her a handful of coins.

At last we were out of this nightmare. We turned right onto Workhouse Lane. I felt all itchy. I wanted to bathe and get changed into clean clothes, but we still had one last call to make. Dora led us to Lizzy's cottage.

She knocked and the uncle answered. The miserable man had the same bit of news, that Lizzy was back at the mill, completing her shift for the day, and he wasn't too eager for all of us to come in, disturbing Timmy. The boy was asleep, which sounded good. I was quite sure he needed some rest. In the end only Dora went in. She stayed about ten minutes and came out pleased to report that the boy's hand was suitably bandaged.

"He won't grow his fingers back," I said.

The curate said there were many folk in the town who had lost hands, arms or legs in similar accidents. "We do our best to find work for them all…"

We had to part ways at this point. The curate said he was needed to go along with the vicar to visit a wealthy widow. Her husband had owned a mill. On his death she had sold it to Father, and now her greatest problem in life was being too lavish with sherry. "But I'll be careful," he promised, giving Dora a peck on the cheek.

Back at The Towers I hastened upstairs. I was feeling quite shaky and troubled. I sat down and wrote a short letter. I popped a silver guinea into the envelope and wrote:

To pay for some medical treatment.

Then I added a little PS:

Why don't we meet tomorrow, at the shack, just like we used to? I could be there after you finish your work. Write back and give your answer to Billy.

Chapter Six

I might have gone out for another ride, but Mother called me in. I was rather relieved when she didn't ask where I'd been with Dora. She thought Dora far too earnest, thanks to 'that frightful curate'. I might have agreed with her over that, but what I had seen in the town had put such thoughts in the shade.

"If only those officers hadn't gone off, they would have been fun," she sighed, "especially for your birthday. I just hope they'll come back as soon as they've stopped those radicals trying to stir up trouble; they really are spoiling the summer."

I promised her I wouldn't get bored over the summer and I'd keep an eye on my sisters. They seemed to be having enormous fun shuffling cards on a pin-board, arranging them into patterns. It looked like a seating plan. "What's that for?" I asked.

They wouldn't explain, but burst into torrents of giggles. This prompted Mother to take my hand and ask me how I liked Louisa. "She seemed to be very impressed with you and all your tales about London."

The girls made strange '*ooh*-ing' noises. Then Emily asked me brightly what I would like for my birthday, which brought further torrents of giggles. After

everything I'd been through today, they all seemed terribly trivial! I needed masculine company.

I found Father in his study. We sat on brown leather armchairs in front of the empty fireplace. He asked for my impressions of what I had seen at the mill. I thought he meant Timmy's accident. I made an eloquent speech about it being more serious than might have been thought at the time. "The poor lad lost three fingers, and actually, Father," – I took the plunge – "I'm worried about the whole family. They haven't got any income, not now, except what Lizzy can earn, which can't be that much, in the loom room?"

Father failed to reply, so I simply carried on about her father being fired for saying a few rash words. "I mean, he was always so loyal. Remember, you gave him a timepiece to thank him for saving the engine the day that valve got blocked. He risked life. Now enough's enough. Don't you think he deserves his job back?"

Father suddenly stirred. "*If* he'd eat humble pie, but he won't; he's still stirring trouble."

"What rot!"

"He's in with those Chartists! They're having a meeting tomorrow, in his cottage"

32

"No, surely not, Father?"

"That shows what you know." He rubbed at his nose. "I have my spies on the look out." And then he went into a rant about how he couldn't leave 'nothing' to chance. He'd built up the mill with hard graft. Iron hand in an iron glove.

And then we had the whole history of how his father had started life as only a common hand weaver, in a family of twelve. How they'd been crammed into one small cottage. Half of them worked the looms in the day, the other six working at nights. The beds had never been cold. And somehow they'd scrimped and saved until they could buy more looms and start to employ other weavers, "Until your grandfather had the brass to invest in his first power loom!" Father tapped the side of his forehead: "That's what I've been building on here, since he died. I want to use the potential of water and coal to maximize production with minimum labour, Josh. That way I cut back on wages. It's a hard world, there's tough competition. But I've kept turning a profit by making men sweat for their pennies. And that's why I'll fight these radicals. Because, if they have it their way, we'll be their slaves, not their masters!" He suddenly seemed to deflate. "Not that you need to worry."

All the anger had drained from his face. For once

he looked friendly and mellow. "I want something better for you, lad. That's why I'll put up with your fancy words, and your poetry books and your nonsense about all the swell folk in London. But leave me to handle Matt Sprott!"

I wasn't sure what to make of Father's talk in the study, though in the morning, I have to admit, I came down to breakfast relieved to think I would not have to go to the mill. I had the whole day to do as I pleased, and I planned to read a whole novel.

That evening I went for a ride on the ridge, enjoying the summer sunshine, ending up outside that old shack. But Lizzy never turned up, and this rather lowered my mood. I rode home, wondering whether she thought me too grand for her now. In many ways this was true, but I wanted to tell her my news, and hear her side of the story concerning her father… and Timmy. Perhaps I should write to her one more time, to tell her she needn't be shy?

Chapter Seven

It was my birthday!

I had a special breakfast, with a beefsteak and three fried eggs. Father didn't join us. Instead he stayed shut in his study. But Mother and all my sisters were there while I opened my presents. For some peculiar reason Emily gave me box containing a pink model pig. "Not a pig, Josh, a sow," she insisted. My younger sisters went, *"Ooooh!"*

A couple of days had gone by since my serious talk with Father. I'd gone up to the shack two nights running but Lizzy hadn't turned up. The more I thought about it the more it seemed most likely she had made up her mind to keep away from me as I was the son of the mill-owner. I can't say I could blame her, especially if her father was really in league with the Chartists.

I spent my birthday morning reading the news in the papers. No wonder Father was sulky, half the mills in the county were empty and bands of ragged men were loose on the high roads and back lanes, living like vagabonds, stealing whatever they fancied.

But something odd was happening at home. Mother wanted me out of the way after lunch, so I went and fished in the lake. And when I came back for

tea I found complete upheaval. The gardeners, with their boots removed, were shifting the furniture. The maids had put up decorations and Lockley was laying the table with Mother's best silver and glass. The air was rich with the smell of slowly roasting meats. Now I guessed why the girls had been busy arranging a seating plan. "Are we having a birthday dinner?"

"A birthday ball!" smiled Emily. "And guess who'll be coming? Loooo-*eeee*-za!"

I wasn't entirely pleased. To make matters worse, when Father came home, with both of us dressed for dinner he called me into his study to give what he called marching orders. He poured himself a large glass of brandy.

He said he wanted to tell me about my stake in the business. This wouldn't involve any daily graft – I could help build the family name. He said, as a capitalist, he'd done his bit, but the next rung up the ladder had to be up to me.

"We only mix with the gentry round here because of your mother's connections. My family had no refinements. That's what I married her for, not for her face. And she married me for my brass. It comes in useful as you'll find out, especially not having to earn it. You see what I'm getting at, Josh, lad?"

I shook my head. This was beyond me.

Father got up and went to the window. "Not yet," he said, peering out, "but give it another five years when you'll have finished your studies, how would you fancy a few months away, going to Paris and Rome? Seeing the sights, travelling Europe with your new wife? I'd be paying."

I stuttered that I couldn't promise, not having a female companion as yet.

"I've sorted that out," declared Father. "I've talked to her father, he's for it. So all you have to do is be nice, make sure she knows how you like her. Be bold, lad. Try it this evening. You can make your first move at the ball!"

I gazed at him in shocked horror, "Who with?"

But I knew the answer already. With a shaking hand I grabbed the glass and swallowed a deep slug of brandy.

The first guests arrived at eight. The mill-owners' wives looked the grandest, arrayed in silk shawls and ball gowns, their jewellery jangling and sparkling in the soft candlelight. Chattering away in loud voices, they talked down to people like Jenks and up to the local gentry, who looked down *their* noses at them as if they couldn't quite manage to admit they were actually here, with 'the commercial classes' as Lady de

Bris might have put it.

I was well-fortified, thanks to that slug of brandy. I wasn't used to such stuff. It had set my insides on fire but it helped when Lady de Bris told me I would be welcome to ride over to Castle de Bris whenever the 'fancy' took me. She was wearing a fusty gown, her blotchy chest ornamented with an enormous pearl necklace and a large ostrich feather. As for Louisa – Loooo-*eeee*-za – her hair had been teased and tonged and topped with a sparkling tiara.

Champagne was poured, glasses raised. As it was still my birthday they all drank to my good health. I needed more fortification myself. When no one was looking I grabbed a glass and downed it as fast as I could. Then Father led the way, escorting Lady de Bris into the dining room where I noticed Emily's seating plan placed me next to Louisa.

Louisa widened her pale blue eyes whenever she spoke to me, and whenever I bothered to answer she leant precariously forward, pretending to be slightly deaf. I knew both my parents were watching. I felt extremely cross. How dare they plan things behind my back and try to manoeuvre me. The whole idea was preposterous. The bubbles had given me hiccups.

As to the food, there was plenty. Soups, fried fishes, roast ducks, a generous saddle of mutton, veal pie and various puddings. Louisa kept asking me questions, but I did my best to ignore her by keeping up conversation with everyone else at the table. The drink had gone to my head. I heard myself spouting forth that the north was backward in matters of taste. I told them all about London.

By the time we got to the fourth course I was not feeling quite so well. In fact I was feeling depressed. I'd not got the sort of reaction a man should expect on his birthday. I suddenly made up my mind to tell them what I'd seen for myself, in the slum that they called Bleekley. Their eyes glazed over. I gave them a shock by reaching out for a glass and helping myself to the claret.

"Josh, no!" said my mother.

I took a deep swig and caught sight of Lord de Bris. Silly man in his dusty grey wig! "I mean, is it fair," I asked him, "that your family lives in a castle when you've never lifted a finger, while others toil night and day to earn a mere pittance? Good Heavens!"

I noticed how quiet it was. Nobody else was talking. Louisa seemed to be looking at me with a very unusual expression. "Papa's not idle," she murmured, "he does grow pineapples, Josh."

I stared at her, not understanding. Then a memory swam into my mind of Lord de Bris in his glasshouse, surrounded by trees and bushes weighed down with exotic fruits…

If only the chandelier would keep still. It was like being on a ship. The whole room seemed to be spinning. Louisa's bosom was wobbling. Trying to fix upon something else, I stared at the window at the far end, only to see pale faces pressing against the glass from outside. I suddenly knew I was drunk.

And the next I knew, there was Lockley, wheeling in a trolley, bearing a giant cake. It was blazing with fifteen candles.

I realized I'd be expected to stand up and blow out the candles. I tried to stand up. It was difficult. I couldn't keep my balance. My legs buckled under me but I couldn't sit down again because Louisa was holding me up, with one arm round my middle. And Emily found this so funny she started to sing Happy Birthday, and everyone else joined in. Rather half-hearted, I thought. They were interrupted by Lockley coming back, whispering something to Father which made Father hold up his hand.

The singing broke off. "Excuse me," he said, and followed Lockley out. Everyone started twittering like birds in the trees about 'trouble'.

I sensed that something was happening.

Then Father was back, he was raising his hands as if to conduct a choir, and everyone started singing 'Happy Birthday' again, in an earnest sort of a way as if they were in a church.

I gazed at all those candle flames, shining gold like a halo. When the time came I gave a great puff, but I must have puffed too high. I only blew out one candle. But as I drew my breath in the dining room door crashed open.

Louisa gave me a terrible squeeze and let out a frightful cry.

A figure swam into focus. A creature in a tattered old dress with a mud splattered hemline and boots. She had messy hair and wild eyes. She was flourishing something. What was it? Some sort of birthday present?

Then Lockley was grappling with her, Father was shouting at them and Louisa's fingernails were cutting into my wrist. The next I knew, there was Lizzy, reading something out as if making a public announcement.

None of this made any sense, it came from too far away. I found my attention was all used up by the way the candle flames flickered, nudged by a draft from the doorway. For some reason Father was ranting again

about her stealing those wretched potatoes.

I tried to object but the words wouldn't form.

I think I passed out after that.

Chapter Eight

Next morning, I had a thick head: my temples were throbbing, I couldn't eat and I was in disgrace. I had let down the name of Grumstone. No matter how bad my headache, Father wanted me down at the mill.

It was hard graft in the outer office, with all the junior clerks scraping away at their ledgers. Jenks was given the thankless task of taking me through the accounts to teach me to balance the books. It was all about inputs and outputs, adding up and subtracting to work out the profit or loss.

"Josh, lad, you've got your eyes shut!"

I opened them. Father glared at me, trundling into a lecture about money not growing on trees. Raw cotton was grown on cotton plants in the American south. It was picked by slaves and shipped across to the great mills of Lancashire. The price of the stuff kept going up. The price of coal went up. But the price for the finished product kept going down for some reason – because of 'intense competition'. Supply was outstripping demand. "It's all about counting the pennies, young man. Somebody has to do it. From now on, you play things my way or you'll end up in this office, totting up figures for Jenks."

Back home I went straight to bed. I was glad to wake up the next morning to find I was free of my headache. Saturday was a half-day at the mill. I hoped I might be let off, but Father insisted we go to the mill so I could carry on having my lesson 'drummed in'.

I had to spend three long hours pretending to go through 'the books'. In fact, I'd brought a new novel to read, and managed to keep it hidden while giving a good impression of being absorbed in a ledger. Thanks to this I was slow to catch on to what was going on across the corridor between my father, Jenks and another two men, all deep in some sombre discussion. But when Father came and told me he had other business to deal with on the far side of town, *ah-ha!*, I thought – here was my chance!

Ten minutes after Father had gone I let myself out of the mill. But instead of taking the high road straight back to Grumstone Towers I cut around a few back roads, coming out onto Workhouse Lane. I was hoping to check on Lizzy, of course. We might not be friends any more, but I wanted to have a talk, not least to ask after Timmy. But as I reached Workhouse Lane, I got a double shock.

Shock number one was my father, mounted, outside Sprott's cottage. I'd have beaten a hasty retreat,

but shock number two came from turning back and seeing an army of men approaching from behind me. These men carried banners and flags, but also axes and cudgels.

I had no choice but to aim for the cottage. As Father swung round in his saddle I noticed the two other men who had come into his office, dumping things outside the porch. Lizzy was by the gate shouting something at Father, and then she was turning on me, as if whatever was happening must be entirely *my* fault! But we had no time for all this. The marchers were closing in fast. At their head was a man in a dowdy black coat. He seemed to recognize Father. There followed an angry dispute. It only came to an end with a deluge of bricks and stones and us making a hasty getaway up the track onto the ridge.

I only worked it all out when we got back to The Towers. Father was furious. Not a man who was usually bettered, he was scheming to get his revenge. His accomplices turned out to be the bailiff and the town constable. They met up in Father's study. The bailiff had blood streaming down his cheek from a gash on the side of his forehead. The constable was breathless, and all he could say, at least four or five times, was that he was 'flabbergasted'.

I asked where the marchers were from, and why they'd arrived in the lane. "For Sprott," spat my father, "they'd come for their man, he's one of the local ring-leaders. We'll go back in force this evening."

"But Father," I said, "you can't take them on, there were hundreds of them. You'd just stir things up!"

"Depends how we fight 'em" snapped Father. "We need to get the Army here, fast."

"There's no hope of that, Mr Grumstone." The bailiff was mopping his brow. "The soldiers are overstretched, I know, in Manchester, keeping down trouble. They won't come here unless things get much worse – with riot and pillage and so forth. Much better just to keep quiet until the mob moves some place else."

Chapter Nine

The following day was Sunday. The marchers had left the town, though as they were camping not far outside it was likely they might return.

On Monday, back at the mill, Father consulted with Jenks. Production had not been affected, though the mood in the mill was uneasy, with discontent being stirred by certain agitators.

"Where's my messenger boy?" growled Father.

Billy entered, flexing his neck. Father quizzed him about what had happened on Saturday afternoon, after 'the bailiff's retreat'. "They were making some plans, sir, I'm certain. But since I've moved in with Mr Jenks, like you told me to, I won't hear much more from now on."

Father sniffed and thought for a moment, staring intently at nothing, drumming his fingers on his desk's green leather top, while I had the sudden alarming thought that I might not have been very wise trusting Billy to take my letters – supposing he told my father? I watched Father handing him money.

"Keep friends with them, go and see them. Find out what Sprott's getting up to. I've got to nab him somehow."

How long had Father been spying on Sprott?

When Billy had gone I told him I could not understand how Sprott could have turned so extreme. "He was always so moderate, Father. We ought to have him on our side."

Father snorted. "How little you know! Get out of here, read the accounts!"

I spent the next hour with Jenks, in his dark, cramped office. I went through more of those ledgers. Not that I concentrated. Apprehension was filling the air, the other clerks were whispering and moving across to the window to peer down onto the street. Until at last Jenks went over and took a quick look for himself. He jerked back with a sharp gasp, and hurried off to tell Father.

I followed, in time to hear him reporting in anxious tones. A crowd was streaming back down the street, gathering outside the mill gates. Then Father was giving instructions for all the doors to be barred and for no one to leave their posts.

I looked down from Father's window. The road was empty again, but the mill yard was now full of people waving banners and flags. Six men were lugging a large wooden beam across towards the doorway.

No sooner had I warned Father than someone

came rushing upstairs, one of the overseers from the cotton store down in the basement.

"Sir, sir, we're being invaded. The men in the bale room have unlocked the doors. The strikers – they're inside the building."

Father charged down the stairs. Jenks and I were close on his heels. We found a great mass of men filling the aisles in the carding room. Reilly was on a soapbox, shaking his fist in the air; reciting his conditions for letting the mill keep working.

"Fair pay for fair work," came the answer, "or else!"

"What else?" shouted Father, above the deafening racket made by all the machinery. "Be grateful for what you've got now or else you'll be out on the street. Ignore this man, he knows nothing!"

"It's you who know nothing," the speaker fired back, jabbing his finger at Father, "nothing about the conditions these people have had to suffer. You have a fine mansion full of fine things, but only because of their labours."

"And who are you, sir, with your Irish voice, to talk on behalf of *my* mill-hands?"

"Their representatives asked me here, to take up their case."

"They've betrayed me, and they will suffer for this, especially that man," Father pointed at Sprott. "I

sacked him, he's no right to be here."

Reilly cupped one hand round his mouth to make sure he would be heard. "Sprott's here to deal with your boilers. You'd like him to take their plugs out, or shall we just brutally smash them?"

"You won't touch my engines!"

"You'll see if we don't. I fear there's no more to be said!"

Then Matthew Sprott was surrounded, hoisted up off the ground by a couple of beefy fellows who carried him off down the aisle, followed by all the throng.

We were left in an empty workspace, the looms still chattering on.

Father ranted and raved at the rafters. He stamped his boots, he turned on Jenks. He promised hellfire and damnation. But then the belts overhead started to run down speed, and slowly, but ever so surely, the looms shunted down to a standstill. The mill was suddenly silent. Then the silence was knocked aside by a huge cheer from outside. And then, without regard for Father or Jenks or myself, the huge crowd of striking miners, along with the whole of our workforce, went squeezing out of the mill yard, like a great snake, down the street.

For the rest of the afternoon my father stayed in his

office, brooding behind a closed door. Jenks was dismissed for the day along with the rest of the staff, the clerks and overseers.

I wandered about by myself, absorbed in the curious silence. I had never been here before without being overwhelmed by the constant, thunderous din. Now the light from those large, hazy windows was strangely bright and clear. Even the dust had settled, forming a furry white coating over the rough, bare floor.

I went out and sat on a bench in the yard. Around me were heaps of grey cotton waste and bunkers piled with coal. Looking up at the tall brick chimney I saw there was nothing more than a wafer-thin strand of smoke twisting out of its fat sooty top. The whole place was dead, like a ghost mill.

And then I got to thinking how this had come to pass. The curious fact that Matthew Sprott had come and disabled our engine. He had always been such a mild man, yet now he was teamed up with Reilly, a firebrand and rabble-rouser. He had done it, I supposed, to get his revenge on Father for wrecking his life.

Chapter Ten

Back home, my sister Dora was in the drawing room. The tea things had been cleared away and Mother had gone to her boudoir to change into her evening gown. I told Dora what had been happening, but she had already heard most of the details, thanks to the vicar coming to tea. Reverend Maple liked our cream scones. "He said it's all because 'evil men' have been here stirring up discord, Catholics over from Ireland!"

"That's how Father likes to see it," I said.

"He's not even taken the trouble to read through their petition."

"I thought it got torn up."

Dora told me she'd saved it, taking it up to her room to stick it together again: "It's only fair what they're asking for, or that's what Bernard says."

"Bernard?"

She went a bit pink. "You know who I mean – Curate Broome. He's made it his mission to study conditions here in the town, Josh."

"You mean on your charity visits?"

"He's writing a paper about it to present to some leading campaigners. Children who work in our mill, Josh, go totally deaf from the noise. The dust gives them lung diseases. Have you noticed how few mill-

hands are over forty years old? Where do you think they all go? They're all dead!"

After dinner I went to the study and found Father back at his desk. I asked him what he intended to do now that the mill was closed. He responded with a contemptuous sneer, pushing a letter towards me. "Billy's just brought this from Reilly. Read it, and give your opinion."

The letter called for a meeting:

This strike will be costing you dearly. You know our demands are just. We suggest the day after tomorrow.

I scanned the list of signatories. Matthew Sprott's name was near the bottom.

"Well, surely you'll go?" I said.

"The other owners would never agree!"

I suggested their positions could be no stronger than ours. I tried to flatter him slightly. "You're a great businessman, Father. Our mill is the biggest in Bleekley. If you say you all need to sit down and talk, they'd listen."

He raised his hands. "I tell you, any concession will only make us look weak. And once we've shown we're weak, lad," he spread his hands out, "more demands. And so on until we're finished. Much better to stall for time."

I took a deep breath. "Don't you think, if we

agreed to improve things, to make their lives a bit better, we'll earn some gratitude from them? Would it really cost all that much?"

He gave a cold-hearted chuckle. "Why should I want to improve things? You think they'd work any harder? I tell you, there's nothing like hunger for making a man rise before five and work fifteen hours every day! Self-interest, the family's interest, what else do you think makes the world turn?"

We waited. The town stayed quiet, and Father stayed sullen, withdrawn. However bullish he liked to appear, he was mourning his loss of production. Every day was costing him dearly. Over breakfast Mother said lightly, "One good thing's come from all this – I don't get woken up by the bell at half past five every morning!"

Dora and I exchanged glances.

According to the newspapers, two hundred representatives of the Trades Associations had met in Manchester. They had come from mills and factories across the north of England to speak out against low wages and vote support for the Charter. As a result, most of Lancashire seemed to have come to a halt.

On the second day, Father went out without saying where he was going. He came back mid-afternoon,

looking a great deal more buoyant than he had done all week, as if he had heard some grand news.

I followed him into his study.

Without any prompting, he told me, "I've met all the other mill-owners. We've made up our minds we shall go to the inn and have a talk with these people."

He noticed my look of amazement.

"You got me thinking, I grant you that – a compromise might be the thing. So at this meeting tomorrow I want you proposing the motion. It wouldn't come natural from me." He sniffed. "Go off, Josh, write a speech. It's your chance to show what you're made of."

I stuttered my thanks. "I shall do my best. But what made you change your mind?"

He waved me away, "Not now, Josh, I've got two more letters to write. Tell Billy, I'll want him to take them."

I did as he asked, finding Billy eating cake in the kitchen. I helped myself to a slice, feeling quite proud of myself, happy to take the credit for Father's great change of heart. I wanted to go and tell Dora! But more important was writing my speech. This way I would win his respect!

I was humming a jaunty tune as I led Billy back to the study, and saw Father give him two envelopes, one

to 'Todd, Town Constable', the other addressed to 'Mr Reilly'.

"You know where to find him?" asked Father.

Billy said he would wait in Workhouse Lane until the man paid Sprott a call. "Don't worry, sir, you can trust Billy."

Father threw him a handful of coins and told him to come back later. "I want to know *anything*, boy."

Chapter Eleven

That evening the constable came, wearing his uniform and his Battle of Waterloo medal. I followed him into the study and sat down in a leather armchair, hoping to hear a bit more. Father turned round with two glasses. The sight of more brandy made me feel sick. He frowned at me. He looked peeved.

"No need for you to be here, Josh. I only asked the constable to talk about keeping the peace while we're inside the George Inn." A foxy glint was in his eye; he was back to his normal self, "Now go off and see to your mother. She's worried about all this upset."

I made a dignified exit, only to slam the door. But I wasn't going to Mother. I had a nagging suspicion that I would be missing something.

I hastened out of the house. I went along the terrace and burrowed my way through some shrubs until I was close enough to smell my father's cigar smoke wafting out of his window. I was lucky that thanks to the long hot day, the sash had been pushed right up to let in some cool evening air.

I needed to shin up a drainpipe to get my chin close to the sill. From here I could hear him rambling on, "We're dealing with a monster here, Todd!" What *was* he talking about? Stuff about cutting its head off,

then talk of 'the common crowd' and 'the mood of the mob'.

"They'd be helpless," he said, "without the brains doing the thinking."

It took me a while to catch on.

"We usually act as the brains, Todd – the owners, we're in control – because we're the ones giving orders and we've got the brass to hand out. But the monster's rebelled and changed its master. In my mill it's Matthew Sprott!"

"So what are you getting at here, sir?"

"We have to lop off the head, Todd. And that's where *you* come in. At the meeting tomorrow."

Todd laughed incredulously. And then, in the silence, I heard a quill pen scraping over paper. I needed to peep through the window. I reached out, grabbed the sill and managed to lean far enough to see Father push a fat envelope across the desk towards Todd. No doubt it was stuffed full of banknotes. But I had leaned out too far. My feet lost their grip on the drainpipe. I went plunging into a bush.

Too winded to try to escape, I lay tangled up in its branches, aware of Father and Todd peering out of the window.

"Most likely a cat," Todd decided.

I heard the sash window slide shut.

As soon as I thought it safe, I got myself out of that bush and crept back into the house, up the stairs to my bedroom. I should have guessed, it was too good to be true that Father should have been willing to sit down as an equal with men he despised and hated. He had to impose himself. He wanted to get Matthew Sprott to make an example of him, I guessed, so the others would bend to his will.

But I was involved in all this. I was meant to be making the speech. How dare Father go behind my back when he said he was relying on me!

I sat down to write a letter.

I had to do several drafts. The first one took half an hour and covered several pages. The last one was only a minimal note, no more than a warning to Lizzy that she should do all she could to keep Sprott away from the meeting. I signed it simply, 'your friend'.

Another hour and the house would be still, with everyone gone to bed. 'Early to bed and early to rise, makes a man healthy, *wealthy* and wise,' as my father was fond of saying. The clock was striking half past ten as I opened my bedroom door.

It took about fifteen minutes to walk to Workhouse Lane. I was lucky that thanks to a clear, full moon it was easy to find my way.

Should I push the letter under the door or leave it

on the front doormat? It had to be Lizzy who found it, so she had time to read it, consider it and decide what to do…

I rummaged about in the vegetable plot, delving for little pebbles. My hands closed round a fat cabbage. I rooted it up, stripped its outer leaves and chucked it up at her window.

It made a soft bump on the sill. I waited but no reaction. I picked it up again and chucked it rather harder than I intended. This time it banged on the pane.

Moments later the window opened and Lizzy's pale face emerged, framed by her fuzzy dark hair. She looked all about; she was still half asleep. I was just about to call her when she looked down at the doorstep and must have caught sight of my letter. She drew back, shutting the window.

I waited. The front door opened. She was wearing a long white nightgown. As she reached out to pick up the letter I stepped forward out of the shadows, overcome with the need to let her know that I was her friend in need. I would have called out, 'It's me, it's Josh – the same Josh you knew last summer!' But her father popped up close behind her.

I stepped back. The front door slammed shut. An owl hooted, then there was silence.

Chapter Twelve

Father and I ate breakfast alone, much earlier than usual so we could set out for the nine o'clock meeting. As we rode into town I was nervous. I had my speech in my pocket. I had written it out and corrected it and written it out again. Determined not to be side-showed by Father's shabby plan I had stayed up most of the night perfecting a fine oration. If this changed the mood of the meeting it should make Father think again!

Should I challenge him now, I wondered? No, that would only annoy him and make things more difficult later.

The High Street was crowded with people. There were townsmen but also strikers, most of them from elsewhere. More than one jeered at the sight of us both, in our smart coats, riding our fine horses. But Father looked over their heads as if they didn't exist. Outside the George Inn, we dismounted. An ostler walked our horses into the yard at the back. Ignoring the taunts and whistles as if they were all directed at somebody else, not himself, Father pushed through the scrum, into the inn. "Right then, Josh, lad, let's cheer up the other mill-owners."

The landlord showed us into a room at the front of

the building. Its window faced out on the street. The diamond-paned glass was thick and pale green, keeping out much of the light. This gave the room a dark, watery feel, as if we were under the sea. Dark shadows passed back and forth outside like monsters in the deep. The other owners got up. They greeted us, shook our hands. We joined them at a long table. There were twelve chairs drawn up on either side, ready for our conference. The air was acrid with pipe smoke. Cartwright, Derby and Huston all looked depressingly glum.

"If this goes wrong we're in trouble, what with that mob," said Huston. "I hope you know what you're doing, putting our lives in danger."

"I have it all planned," said Father. "You don't have to lift a finger."

"I'm sure it's all fine," I said brightly. "My motion will put them at ease. It's what they've been hoping for, after all – a chance to thrash out our differences. They're not all unreasonable men."

"Are they not?" Cartwright squinted at me, as if I was some sort of insect. I remembered the last time he'd seen me, slumped over my birthday cake, and felt my composure weakening. In fact I was very relieved when the landlord popped his head round the door to say that the strikers' leaders had just arrived in a group.

We heard their loud, cocky voices out in the corridor. I listened hard to try to catch Sprott's voice, but if he was there he kept quiet.

"Show them into the room at the back," Father said. "We've still got a bit more discussing to do, to fix on our opening offer. We'll ask them to join us shortly."

"It'd better be good," called Reilly.

As soon as the door clicked shut I reckoned the time had come to tell everyone here at the table what I intended to say. But as I drew out my notes and asked if they would be happy to have me give them a read through, Father raised a finger as if to warn me to be quiet.

In the silence we all heard Reilly, through the wooden partition, maintaining a jaunty banter. The other leaders seemed more subdued, but grudgingly laughing back, as if not so sure of themselves. Then I heard what sounded suspiciously like a hefty iron key rattling into a lock. Reilly must have heard it too. Moments later the catch was rattled, a fist thumped hard on the door and Reilly was shouting out, demanding to know what was happening. Then Father got to his feet, speaking under his breath, "Before the rumpus begins, my friends, let me tell you their room at the back has another doorway opening

into the yard. They'll be leaving that way fairly promptish."

Next moment, this 'rumpus' began. I heard a loud crash, angry cries, and exhortations from the constable not to resist but 'come quiet'. Then much more clattering, thumps and yells. I heard furniture overturned. Bodies banged into the thin wooden wall. And then a peculiar silence.

"What on earth… ?" I was up on my feet but Cartwright, Huston and Darby stayed in their seats, heads down. Only Father looked fully at ease – in fact he looked almost merry. His voice sounded jaunty and sure.

"The constable's got a coach in the yard. The coachman has his instructions to drive fast for Manchester Gaol. Those scoundrels will soon be under arrest. They'll be charged with damaging property and disturbing the public peace. They can do their blasted talking with the magistrates, not with us."

"If the coach gets away through the crowd," Darby said, not sounding too hopeful about it, "this will stir up a hornet's nest, Grumstone!"

Father chuckled. "You don't have to worry. The yard opens onto a lane at the back, so the coach can avoid all the crowds. I suggest we leave now the same way. We should have twenty minutes before the alarm

goes up. By then, it'll be too late. The monster's lost its head, thank God. In other words, it will be dead!"

We all moved as one to get out. None of us shared Father's faith in the monster now being dead. If the crowds in the street got a hint of what had just happened inside, they might string us all up from the lampposts.

I had misunderstood Father's plan, thinking he'd be satisfied with only bagging Sprott. He'd taken a much bigger gamble. But had he been shrewd and cunning or merely reckless and stupid?

"You betrayed me as well," I told him. "I sat up all night trying to get my speech right – and you never even intended to give me the chance to persuade them."

"Pah!" Father mounted his horse. "This is the real world, Josh. What matters is getting results."

"Depends what they are!"

"Wait and see. I'll wager the mill will be working again before the end of the week!"

We had to trot down the lane behind the constable's coach. I was thinking it wasn't so easy to tell how the crowds might react, any more than I could see clearly through the clouds of white dust raised by the coach's iron-shod wheels. Then a figure

emerged from the haze up ahead. Her face was partly wrapped in a shawl. She drew into a gateway to let the coach past but ever so briefly our eyes met. It was Lizzy – where was she going? Had she left her father at home or had he turned up for the meeting?

I watched the coach swing round the bend, back onto the Manchester road, wondering who was inside it. Then I saw the coach window fly open. A head popped out. It was Reilly. He moved remarkably fast. One moment his arm was reaching up, his hand grabbing hold of the roof rail; the next, he had pulled himself over the sill. Then his legs were dangling free. They paddled about, then he let himself drop, coming down on the road. He stumbled and lost his balance. He went somersaulting over.

Father was shouting, spurring his horse, as if to ride the man down. But the constable got in the way. Todd tried to rein his horse round to grab at Reilly's collar. But the Irishman was too nifty. Springing up on his feet he seized the constable's wrist, and with an extraordinary tug, pulled him out of his saddle.

I watched as if in a dream, the constable's horse veering round, Reilly taking a jump, landing with one foot in the stirrup. And snatching hold of the bridle, he spurred the horse through a gateway, out across an

open field before anyone else could have stopped him.

Chapter Thirteen

Afterwards, back at Grumstone Towers, Father held a council of war. He was furious, spitting with rage. He was trying to find a scapegoat and railing at me as a coward, a useless slow-witted coward who ought to have chased after Reilly.

As for the constable, he was in pain. He had a twisted ankle and bloody bruise on his forehead. He'd had to be given a ride in a pony and trap from the mill. Now Dora was cleaning the wound while the constable mumbled, "At least only one rogue escaped."

"Aye, we've got Sprott," growled my father.

Dora stopped dabbing the wound. I held my breath. Todd pulled a face. He cleared his throat. "No, we have not, sir."

Father scowled, "What does *that* mean?"

"It means that I did what you asked, sir, arresting every one of the scum that was with Reilly in the back room. But Sprott wasn't in the back room, sir. He never turned up to the meeting."

Father sniffed. "So where is he?"

Todd considered. "His cottage? *Your* cottage, speaking correctly."

I risked a glance at my father, expecting another

wild outburst, but his eyes had a distant gaze, as if he was calculating: "Why would Sprott have not been at the meeting? He had every reason to be there, unless… someone warned him off, Todd."

"Like who, sir?" Todd sounded defensive.

Silence: I looked elsewhere. I felt the blood pulsing hard in my neck. I was waiting for him to accuse me. It proved a long wait. No one dared interrupt. But at last he nodded his head. "That messenger boy," he said quietly. "The brat took my letter to you, Todd. Supposing he steamed it open, found out that I'd asked you up here and come back to hear our discussion: Remember that noise outside, eh? It wasn't a cat − it was *him*, listening in through the window."

"No, sir, I can't think."

"Who else then?"

Dora got to her feet. Her eyes were like glass. "Maybe no one: it's perfectly possible, Father, Matthew Sprott had personal reasons for keeping away from your meeting."

"Oh? What might they be?"

"Bernard told me…"

"Bernard? Who's Bernard?"

"The curate. As you well know, Father. Bernard told me some very sad news − that Matthew Sprott's son has died. It happened two days ago."

This was the first I had heard, "The same day the mill was invaded?"

But Father was off on a tangent. His devious mind had moved on to trying to calculate how he could gain from this. "If Reilly's on the run, Todd, he'll head for Sprott's cottage. So this is our chance. We'll get them both. Send your men round. Get them to hide, watch the place."

"I've not got the men for a fight, sir. Reilly will still have supporters. They'll rally round. They'll protect him. I'm worried enough, I can tell you, what with safe-guarding the mills in the town. There's no chance of us getting soldiers, they're too overstretched in the city. And then there's this house. Have you thought, sir, how you might try to defend it? I think you should plank up the windows."

Father barely had time to pour scorn on all this before Lockley peered round the door, looking as solemn as ever, to tell us that Lady de Bris had arrived, "Quite unexpectedly, sir. She wants to see you in person. Should I tell her you're rather busy?"

No chance: she was barging past him, with Louisa close behind, looking red-faced and flustered. "Mr Grumstone, you've not heard the news – about my unfortunate husband?"

"How should I have done?" snapped Father.

"What's he done now? Lost his wig?"

"Papa's been kidnapped!" wailed Louisa, and both of them burst into tears.

We had to sit them down on the brown leather sofa. Dora provided clean hankies and Lockley brought sweet tea. We got the news out of them, bit by bit, that several hundred strikers had set up camp in their park. The strikers had bathed in the lake, ripped branches off the trees, lit fires, plundered vegetable gardens and stolen chickens and eggs from the poultry house. And then had broken into the hothouse to pick the exotic fruits. For Lord de Bris this had been the last straw. Taking his blunderbuss, he had sallied forth out to confront them and hadn't been seen again.

"We heard two loud bangs but, oh dear, Josh!" Louisa grabbed my wrist. "We sent a servant to see who he'd shot, but she couldn't find any bodies. Papa hasn't come back though. They must have got him and taken him off. Oh please, you've got to help us!"

I pledged to do what I could, but what could I do?

"Fetch the Army!" demanded Lady de Bris.

Father stuttered about the Army not having the men to save Manchester, let alone Lord de Bris. And Louisa started crying again, leaning closer to keep my attention, with help from her rather low neckline.

I had to get out of this place. I was still thinking of poor, dead Timmy, still thinking about poor Lizzy. And here was my chance to escape. I claimed I would try my best to find His Lordship and bring him back dead or alive and, hopefully in the process, I might prove to my father I wasn't the coward he'd called me!

With that, I hastened out, closely followed by Dora. She grabbed my hand in the hallway. "Josh, what are you going to do?"

I said I'd ride over to Castle de Bris, but first I would go to Sprott's cottage. I needed to talk with Lizzy. "I wish I'd gone days ago!"

It was twilight out on the ridge. The heather was catching the last of the light, radiating purple against the emerald green bracken. The atmosphere was heavy and stale, still full of the heat of the day.

It should have been peaceful and quiet. Instead, from the top of the ridge, I could hear distant shouts and cries, breaking glass and shuddering noises, as if whole rooftops of tiles were cascading down into the streets. I could see several houses burning, black smoke rolling into the sky. The headless monster was angry, not dead. I rode on down the hill, wondering how this could end well.

The Army was far away. Our mill might be razed

to the ground. Was it too late to try to prevent this? What if I reached the cottage and found the Irishman Reilly being sheltered by Matthew Sprott? Would either of them want to meet me? Supposing we talked things through? I wondered if it would show respect if I said that Timmy's death ought to make us all think again – to make good come out of bad?

Could the Army bring the mob back into line? If the mill-owners all agreed to get the strikers' leaders released from Manchester Gaol, could we all sit down at a table and come to some shared agreement? Both sides would lose from a conflict, so why was it unrealistic to want a fair compromise?

I found myself in Workhouse Lane. I found myself outside the cottage. I found myself striding up to the door, and knocking, and waiting, and knocking. Then I gave the door a slight push and realized it was open. I walked inside – nobody there.

Chapter Fourteen

The Sprotts had gone. Yet the kettle was warm. They'd not been gone more than an hour. I should have been depressed, though in a way I felt glad, because it made me think they had wanted to get away from here – as a family, rather than wait for Reilly and get involved with his mob. This meant that I'd been right to write that letter to Lizzy. But then I realized I'd probably missed my last chance to meet up with Lizzy and try to make friends again. No doubt she had gone away thinking I was a spoilt fop – and Father's unthinking heir. And maybe I was, or I had been. Now I was caught, without any choice, in this mess my father had made. If need be, what else could I do but help defend my family against his 'headless monster'.

Or that was how I was thinking as I rode back past the gates to The Towers and on down the Manchester road, aiming for Castle de Bris.

It took about twenty minutes. The castle was really a stately home built in the 1720s on the site of a ruined castle. It had stone pillars along the front like an Italian villa and faced out over a lake. The tall Georgian windows were dark. There was no sign of strikers or campers anywhere in the park. I went

round the back, past the stables, determined to look in the hothouse, if only to find some ripe fruit.

Although it was nearly dark, the twilight reflected across the ground in thousands of glinting stars. It was littered with broken glass. My boots crunched over the fragments. And inside the hothouse I rapidly saw that the place had been totally pillaged. The thieves had been ruthless and careless, stripping all fruits from the vines and the trees. There were only a few squashed apricots smeared on the green tiled floor. The robbers were all long gone, I guessed. But as I moved past a pineapple palm, I heard something click. I looked round. A pistol was aimed at my face.

"Don't move, just say who you are."

The voice sounded educated which helped me relax enough to answer the question calmly. But I still felt a great deal better seeing the pistol lowered. A man stepped out of the darkness. He was wearing a red uniform. He held out his hand. "Pleased to meet you. I went to Grumstone Towers more than once while we were camping here. You must be Emily's brother, young Josh! I'm Giles Muldoon – has Emily mentioned me? I'm lieutenant in the Fourth Horse. She told me all about you. In fact, I'd been hoping to meet you, but then we got orders to march. We've been around Manchester ever since then, marching

from pillar to post, trying to turn up everywhere to give the mob the impression there's more of us than there are. It's worked so far, more's the pity – we've not had to open fire once!"

"But why are you back here?" I asked him.

He told me he had come back here on behalf of Captain Bulmer. "The fellow's gone soft on Louisa. Wanted a letter delivered, asking Lord de Bris for his daughter's hand in marriage! Can't understand it myself, but there, I volunteered for the mission, hoping I might get the chance to slip along to your place, see Emily for ten minutes. But then I got here, saw this mess. I can't think what's happened. Do you know?"

I filled him in on the details. "It keeps getting worse," I told him. "I'm worried they'll burn our mill down."

"We can't have that, Josh. We must stop it."

"If only…"

"I'm serious though." And in a most serious way, he told me that Captain Bulmer would be mad keen to avenge Castle de Bris being ransacked, in order to honour Louisa. "But we'd have to persuade the colonel to give us the order to march!" And in a most urgent way, he said the best way to play this was with a request from my father, explaining the dire

situation, so Colonel Ackridge could justify heading south first thing, to bring back law and order. "But hold on, where's Lord de Bris?"

Good question. We spent twenty minutes going our separate ways, calling out to His Lordship. But only when we met up again, outside the hothouse doorway, did we hear a low, worried whimper from somewhere behind, in the darkness. Muldoon struck a match, and as it flared, I saw a pale face with glazed eyes peering nervously out from under a black tarpaulin that covered a heap of manure. We helped him up on his feet. His Lordship had lost his wig. He was bald. He was plastered in pig manure.

"I th-thought I'd be stuck there forever," he gasped. "The stench! I could hardly bear it. It did prove a safe place to hide though. Not where your average ruffian would look for a lord of the realm!"

Muldoon headed back to his regiment to give the colonel our news while I returned to Grumstone Towers with Lord de Bris riding pillion. He was holding onto my waist from behind. His teeth were chattering away less than an inch from my ear, but even so, he told me how he had got in that mess: his blunderbuss had backfired, "It kn-knocked me clean off my feet, into the horrible muck bin. Just my luck, as it happened. I'd never have chosen to hide there."

At The Towers I was welcomed back like a conquering hero. I got a wet kiss from Louisa and a strenuous hug from her mother. "For this you are forgiven, young man, for how you behaved on your birthday!"

When I told them about my meeting with Lieutenant Muldoon, this cheered them up no end. Jenks and Todd shook my hand. As Father wrote to the colonel I turned back to see Louisa gazing at me, wide-eyed, with what I could only describe as open admiration. "You like Captain Bulmer?" I hinted. "He'll leap at the chance to help *you*."

"And so he should too," growled Father, glaring up from his desk. "The strikers are holding a meeting tomorrow, outside the mill gates. If Colonel Ackridge can get his men here in time for midday, he'll catch that rascal Reilly before he can stir up more mischief. We'll just have to hope Sprott will be there. I gather he's fled from my cottage!"

"Who told you that Sprott had gone, Father?"

Father's voice had an ominous edge. "My so-called messenger boy was up here half an hour back. I told him what I suspected – that he must have been the scoundrel who warned Sprott about that meeting. Somebody must have done it! That made him wriggle and squirm, I must say. Then the nasty wretch tried to

blame you. Said he had letters to prove that you were so soft on Sprott's daughter that you'd betray your own father! Of course, it was all empty bleating. I cuffed the brat, told him to leave and never come back to the mill unless he could track down Sprott. In which case he'd receive a bumper reward. That ought to work wonders, I reckon!"

Chapter Fifteen

I had an uneasy night, wondering if my letters had ever been delivered. If not, if Billy decided to hand them in to my father, I could be in great trouble. I'd have to get hold of him and bribe him to give the letters back to me, but that would have to wait. I set off soon after dawn, on my mission to Colonel Ackridge.

Even before I left, the carpenters were busy, boarding up downstairs windows. Lockley was bossing the gardeners. They had turned out with pitchforks and scythes, to mount a guard at the gates. But these were just token precautions, for fear of the mob arriving before I returned with the soldiers.

The journey took two hours longer than it ought to have done. This was thanks to me making wide detours round towns and larger villages, and keeping well clear of people moving about in large groups. But nobody got in my way and it was a good enough ride, mostly across open country. It was cool in the early morning, and I had some time to think about what I was doing – an awful thing and no mistake – to bring the Army to Bleekley to stamp down our very own mill-hands. But the choice was

either that or our mill burning down. It didn't seem much of a choice.

The camp was on Heddington Moor, a short way out of the city. I arrived there about eight o'clock. A cluster of white canvas bell tents had been put up in a low hollow, either side of the gravelled toll road. Horses were tethered under some trees and camp fires were smoking away, warming up black iron kettles. A regimental flag hung droopily from a white pole. The scene was peaceful, a world away from the mobs rampaging in Bleekley.

Dismounting, I called to some soldiers, asking for Lieutenant Muldoon. He emerged from a tent with white shaving froth all over his cheeks and chin. I handed him a short letter Emily had written, adding her tuppence of pleading, then showed him my other letters – from Father to Colonel Ackridge.

The colonel was eating his breakfast of sausages and fried bacon. When I told him what brought me here he asked me to sit down and join him. And after he'd finished his plateful he sat back and read Father's letter, then looked up, with a wide grin. "Our chance for some action, hey, chaps?"

It took time to summon the men, to get them on parade, buckled up ready to march. The horses had to be saddled, the officers had to get into full dress, and

then the colonel needed to give them his marching orders – two columns with separate routes. He wanted a pincer movement, to enter the town from both ends.

I thought we'd ride back at full speed, scattering dogs and hens. But we had to go at a slow, sluggish trot with regular stops on the way, because of the infantry marching behind. Only a trio of horsemen acting as forward scouts went galloping on ahead and over the hills either side, jumping hedges and ditches and signalling down from high outcrops. The rest of us stuck to the road, stomping up a great dust cloud that got into the eyes and hair. I feared we might all be too late.

By the time we set out on our final stretch down the straight length of road that led past Grumstone Towers it was nearly midday. Several gardeners were outside the gates on guard, and as we galloped the last hundred yards, three other horsemen emerged from the gates, the constable, Jenks and my father.

"You fools are late," cried my father. "I'd given up hope of you coming. I thought you'd deserted us, lad, and joined up with my enemies!"

"Father?" There was something about his chill tone of voice that told me this wasn't a joke. This was confirmed as I caught sight of Billy on the far side of his horse, watching me intently.

"The spy in our midst," said Father, not looking at Billy but me. And when I asked what *that* meant, he pulled three envelopes from the inside of his jacket and flapped them under my nose. All three were addressed to Lizzy.

"Sir, you don't understand…"

"Do I not?" He took a sheet of paper out of one of the envelopes. "You wrote this to warn her father to stay away from the meeting. It couldn't be clearer. Billy was right, and there I was, trying to blame him. You lacked the guts to be honest you coward! Now what do you say?"

I took a deep breath and I tried to explain, how Matthew Sprott was a good man whose daughter had once been my friend, but Father interrupted stating that she was a thief, and what did I think I was doing, when I could have bided my time and ended up with a fiancée as fair as Louisa de Bris? It was useless for me to deny it. He kept shouting at me, his face bulging. The veins on his temples were popping. There was froth on his lips as he bellowed, "I say you've betrayed flesh and blood, not only me, you scoundrel, your mother and all your sisters! You think you're so clever and smart, I know. You think you're so *intellectual* – but I can still make you regret this. Because you're worth NOUGHT without me, because I can change my

will and…"

He never finished the sentence. His gaze went suddenly rigid, as if something frightening had struck him. He tilted forward, his hand to his chest. And slowly he toppled sideways, into my arms.

I held on. I tried to stop him from falling, but his horse took fright and moved forward, making him tilt from his saddle. Then everyone else gathered round us, trying to help him down, with Jenks leaping down from his pony, grabbing hold of the bridle. Even Billy, still on the far side, detached Father's boot from the stirrup.

We lugged him across to the verge. We laid him back on the grass. He was staring up into the sky. His lips were blue. He kept talking, though only to Colonel Ackridge, insisting the troops march straight into town because there was no time to waste. The mill was under threat. "No mercy," he gasped. "Get the leaders."

"A pleasure, sir," murmured the colonel.

Father's hand was still on his heart. His whole expression contorted as if from a pain in his chest. His hand twitched, fingers opening, revealing a bunch of keys – the keys to the mill. I took them. Next moment he gave a great shudder, and then he was still, and his eyes bulged. I waited, but nothing else happened.

Jenks leant closer, using his fingertips to gently close Father's eyelids. Only then did I know he was dead. It was a shock, a horrible shock, but I felt completely numb. I heard my own voice, from a distance, ordering the gardeners to carry him back down the drive. And I told Jenks to go ahead, to raise the alarm at the house.

Meanwhile the column of soldiers was marching past, on down the road, leaving the mounted officers gathered on the far verge, waiting behind for the Colonel. He took off his hat to show his respect. He gave me a hasty salute. Then he rode off to join his men.

So I was left with Billy. I was too stunned to speak for a while, so many things in my mind. But Billy had been the cause of all this – my father's fatal rage. I had to confront him somehow. So I brought out those letters again. I held up the first two in front of his face, as Father had done with me. "You didn't deliver these, did you?" He offered no answer. I said, "Or did you deliver them for me, then get them back from Lizzy? Did you have to steal them, Billy?"

I waved the third letter under his nose. "And this: speak, how did you get this? I know she got this one, I saw her picking it up off her step, so why is it here now, Billy? Tell me, come on quick, open your mouth. Or I'll have to beat it from you!"

"You ask lots of questions," said Billy, his narrow eyes darting about, "but it's not how you think, Master Grumstone."

"And how do I think?" How much could I think? My head was still reeling with shock from Father's aggressive attack followed by his collapse. I was trying to work out what to do, to follow his body back to The Towers or take my place with the colonel. But Billy was speaking again.

"I know you think I'm worthless. Just a humble little orphan. I have to grub for my pennies. But I've been doing my duty, Master Josh, whatever your father told me – just trying to do my job, don't you see… and that wasn't always easy."

"You don't mean my father told you not to deliver the letters? He can't have known, not at the time?"

"No, oh no. It's just that I couldn't deliver them."

"Why?"

"It went against all my… own feelings."

I stared at him. "You talk of feelings? What about me? How do you think she'd have felt, not hearing anything from me? Not even after the accident when Timmy was ill? But I sent her the funds to call in a doctor to help him!"

"I made sure she did get the money. He did see the doctor, I promise."

"She must have thought I didn't care!"

"I didn't look at it that way."

Now I was ready to hit him. "So how did you *look at it*, Billy?"

He looked at the ground, then looked up. He looked at me straight and he swallowed. "I've been Lizzy's friend all this time, Master Josh, while you were away down in London. I've been with her during the bad times. I was there when her father got sacked. I helped them keep food on the table. I did my best, cheering her up. Then you come swanning back like a prince, back from your good times in London. You think you dash off a note, telling her when to meet you, as if it's some big favour, but that was you playing your games."

"What do you mean, *playing games*?"

His gaze remained steady. "Your future's elsewhere, Master Grumstone. You'd never have cared, not like I did. So what I thought was, if the letters got lost, you'd probably soon forget her. You'd go back to London, you'd have lots of friends. You'll marry Louisa one day."

"I certainly won't!" I retorted. I glared at him, full of contempt. Then another thought crossed my mind. "Do you mean to say Lizzy likes *you*? I mean... you don't hold any hopes that, looking ahead to the

future, you and she...? No, of course not. Preposterous!"

"Lizzy's too good for me," he said sadly.

"So why did you...? What I mean is..." I was exasperated. "Why did you have to show Father that letter I sent warning Matthew Sprott not to go to the meeting? Did you hate me so much? Tell me, Billy."

Billy looked furtive again, less sure of himself, more confused. His voice had a stumbling tone as he told me how Lizzy had thought the letter had come from him, not me, so she'd not minded giving it back. "And your father blamed me, Master Josh, as you know." Billy licked his dry lips. "You'd not got the nerve to own up though. You left me to get into trouble. And when I tried to deny it was me, Mr Grumstone accused me of lying. I had to prove that I wasn't. I did it to get my job back."

I let this pass. "And what about now? Do you know where the Sprotts have gone?"

He pointed up at the ridge.

"What do you mean by that, Billy?"

"That's where they rested the night, sir."

"And now?"

"Now it makes me feel bad, but I've got an admission to make. I've put Lizzy's dad in great danger."

"You mean you told my father?"

"More than that. Worse than that." Billy told me how he had been to the shack, persuading Matthew Sprott to go down into the town, to speak at the meeting with Reilly. "But that was to do some good, not hurt him." Billy grasped my wrist. He looked desperate. "I wouldn't have done it, I promise, if I'd known the Army was coming. I just thought he'd speak for the moderates, and maybe help save the mill."

I wasn't sure if I believed him or not, but just shook my head. He was right about one thing – Lizzy's dad was in great danger.

"Come on," I cried. "No time to waste!"

Chapter Sixteen

I galloped along the Manchester Road with my horse's hooves throwing up dust and pebbles. I turned along a side road and came out in Workhouse Lane, then took a back route down into the town, following narrow alleys. In the confines I slowed to a canter, and now I could hear other horses clattering on the cobbles. I glanced back and caught sight of Billy, gradually catching up, riding on Jenks's pony.

The High Street was strangely quiet, though I could hear a great murmuring roar from somewhere just out of sight, like the sea crashing into the shore at night. Round a corner I saw the soldiers. Their officers mounted on horseback were up on the right, swords drawn, in a file down the street. Colonel Ackridge was at their head. The soldiers on foot had been drawn up in front, broadside across the street. They were holding the crowds at bay with the tips of their bayonets. On the colonel's orders they began to advance, step by careful step. They were steadily pushing forward, forcing people back.

There were must have been five or six hundred crammed into that open space. On their left were the tall stone walls of the mill, followed by a low parapet with the gushing millstream behind it. On their right

was another wall, less tall, but backed by other buildings. On the far side, I guessed, more soldiers were blocking the other way out, preventing any retreat. Reilly's 'meeting' was still in session, with a second speaker addressing the crowd, raised up on somebody's shoulders. I saw who it was – Matthew Sprott. He had an impressive, clear baritone voice that carried his full conviction. And the mill had not been attacked yet – not even a window broken.

The mill gates were closed, the yard empty. I had the keys in my pocket.

This only occurred to me when Ackridge unrolled a parchment. He was going to read out the Riot Act. And then he would be entitled by law to do whatever he liked, 'in order to keep the peace'.

I knew what Father had asked him to do. I knew what the outcome would be. And time was not on my side. With a few shouted words aimed at Billy, I reined my horse round and retreated, dodging the few baffled stragglers standing about on the cobbles. I rode round the side of the mill. I came to the smaller gateway on the far side of the mill. I feared that bolts would be closed from within, but as soon as the lock was turned the heavy oak door swung back and I was inside the yard. It was quiet in here and sheltered; the crowd but a distant murmur. I rode across to the main

double gates, dismounted and drew back both bolts. I turned another large key and the gate on my right creaked inwards. I wasn't a moment too soon.

"FIRE!" bellowed Colonel Ackridge.

The soldiers unleashed a twin broadside, followed a moment later by an answering broadside from the opposite side.

Smoke billowed out. People tumbled. And in that same split second I saw Reilly lose his balance and tumble down from his soapbox. I saw Matthew Sprott veer backwards, arms paddling out at his sides. And there, in the midst of the crowd, I suddenly caught sight of Billy, struggling and shouldering forwards, attention fixed on where Sprott had gone down. He got there. Small but determined, he grabbed hold of Sprott by the shoulders and did his best to drag him back towards the gateway. Soon other men were helping.

Intending to try to give cover, I hastily mounted my horse and spurred her out into the crowd. But from this height I saw Lizzy. I saw her the moment she fell. She must have tripped over a body. She carried on, down on all fours, trying to pull herself up. Then Ackridge roared, "Tally-ho!"

His men came charging forward. The colonel was at their head, his horse prancing into the crowd with

scant regard for anyone ending up under his hooves. He was slashing his sword back and forth. He swept past and wheeled around. He cut down Reilly with one vicious blow. Blood spurted up in a red fountain. And then he must have seen Sprott. His sword swung up again. At the next thrust he'd cut down Billy, opening the way to get Sprott. But Lizzy threw herself at him, grabbing his boot in his stirrup. He knocked her away with the hilt of his sword. And as she reeled back, falling down, throwing up both hands to shield herself from a wild slash, I spurred my horse in between them. I grabbed her and pulled her upwards.

I pulled her up off her feet. She came up over my saddle. I sent her head over, arms and legs kicking out either side, but she was safe like this, cushioned against my horse's mane. Ackridge left her to me.

I glanced around. Soldiers on foot were pressing steadily closer, forcing back terrified people – women, children, old men. Miners and burly mill-hands were doing their best to fight back, wielding their picks and cudgels. But thanks to the gates being open, the rest were able to make an escape, across the yard to safety. I needed to get right away.

Chapter Seventeen

The soldiers allowed me through. They thought I had taken a prisoner.

At last I was out of the crowd, heading back up those alleyways, out along Workhouse Lane and up the hill onto the ridge. I knew where I wanted to take her, back to our shepherds' shack.

The door was unlocked, her uncle inside, along with the little twins.

I helped her down and I carried her in. I lay her down on the straw. But she wasn't going to lie there like a poor wounded victim. She pushed me aside and she sat up straight, looking at me, quite hostile, her lower lip jutting out. She wanted to know if her father was safe, so I told her how Billy had saved him. A shadow of doubt seemed to cross her face as if she knew about Billy and how he'd betrayed us both. So then I started to tell her about the letters I'd written, the guinea to pay for the doctor, only to break off and shake my head, aware this now counted for nothing, compared to the fact we were safe.

"Poor people," she murmured. "So many were hurt."

"My father is dead though," I blurted.

"Dead? But how did that happen?"

I remembered his throbbing veins and blue lips, his threat to disinherit me for going against his orders. I told her all this and I told her much more, going right back to that moment in the potato field when he had attacked her for stealing. ''I understand why you were doing that now. I've learnt a great deal,'' I told her. ''Far more in the last two weeks than I learnt all my time down in London.''

She nodded. ''Me too. Even so....''

There was something about the way she said that which sounded so sad. ''What do you mean?''

She winced at me. ''Think about it. You're still free to go back to London. I've lost my little brother. My father's still out of a job. I'm out of a job, and to make things worse, we've now got nowhere to live.''

This took me aback. But it didn't take long. I knew what I wanted to do. I grabbed her hand and I squeezed it. My father was dead — I was heir to the mill — he'd not lived to change his will! Jenks might have to manage the place, at least for the next few years, but I could be giving some orders.

''I promise,'' I said, ''things will change from now on. I'm going to make things much better. I want your father to have his job back, and you can work too, if you like. So that way you'll still have the cottage. I'm going to get Dora and Curate Broome to

write a list or proposals to try to improve conditions. To start with we'll open a school at the mill and the children can work shorter hours. And we'll have a proper medical man. And the mill shop will sell cheap food. We'll make Grumstone Mill the best mill in the north, an example for all the others!"

She spluttered with laughter.

"What's wrong with that?"

"Oh, nothing." She shook her head solemnly, but she was still smiling strangely. "It's just that you haven't changed, not at all. You've still got your head in the clouds!"